THE STEPPE WOLVES

Punishment Battalion Series
Book Three

Charles Whiting
writing as
K N Kostov

SAPERE
BOOKS

THE STEPPE WOLVES

Published by Sapere Books.

24 Trafalgar Road, Ilkley, LS29 8HH

saperebooks.com

ISBN: 978-0-85495-593-0

Of all man's miseries, the bitterest is this: to know so much and to have control over nothing.

Herodotus

PRELUDE

The sniper crouched in the snow-filled shell-crater and watched the scene, his telescopic rifle at the ready. Behind the crater, Stalingrad burned.

There was something very strange about the bigger 'stick', as the sniper always called the victims: sticks to be cracked — by one steel slug through the brain. He was obviously badly hurt, the sniper could see that well enough. Both he and another stick had survived the crash, injured either by the flak shell which had struck their little Fiesler Storch on the other side of the River Volga or by the impact of the plane smashing into the tight grove of snow-heavy firs. But their terribly slow movements as they staggered about the smoking wreckage of the high-winged courier plane indicated that they were in a bad way.

The sniper chuckled noiselessly. Hardly worth wasting a couple of slugs on the fascist pigs! Still, a sniper had to record ten 'kills' per day if he wanted to be entitled to the 'special hazardous duty' ration and, above all, the precious 100 grammes of vodka, the only thing which made life bearable in the hell of Stalingrad.

The Fritz with the leather helmet, obviously the pilot, began laboriously to unwind a long roll of toilet paper, one end dipped in the wrecked plane's petrol tank. He carried his burden as if it were tremendously heavy, while the bigger of the two watched, one hand on the pistol at his side, the other trying, in vain, to staunch the bright scarlet blood which jetted from a gash in his neck. For a few moments, the sniper's thin face under the heavy fur cap wrinkled in a frown. What was the Fritz up to?

The pilot staggered to a stop and began to fumble with a cigarette lighter with cracked frozen fingers. Of course. He was trying to set fire to his plane! The sniper stared intently through the circle of calibrated glass so that the cross-wires bisected the pilot's head. It would be as easy as falling off a log. The stationary pilot made a perfect target. *'Yer bohi, revenge is in God's hands'* the sniper whispered, uttering the motto of all the Red Army's snipers at the moment of the kill, for then, the sniper himself was God.

The paper ignited. The pilot dropped it carefully into the snow and stood there, swaying slightly, as the purple flame ran swiftly along the roll of paper towards the open petrol tank.

The sniper closed one eye. Grip hard on the stock, tuck butt firmly into shoulder, tight and firm. *First pressure...* The pilot was outlined a clear, stark black in the circle of gleaming glass... *Second pressure...* Breathing slow and relaxed, the sniper whispered, 'Now, fascist —' the words died abruptly on the sniper's lips.

One hundred metres away, the bigger of the two sticks had pulled out his pistol. Calmly, very deliberately, he placed the muzzle at the base of the unsuspecting pilot's skull. In the same moment that the plane exploded in a great rending crash, instantly engulfed in greedy yellow flames, he pulled his trigger.

The back of the pilot's head disintegrated. Thick flurries of blood sprayed the killer, covering the front of his elegant staff-officer's uniform. Instinctively the sniper, shocked by this strange, cold-blooded assassination, squeezed the trigger. The butt kicked back hard. Suddenly the winter air stank of burnt cordite. To the front, the officer, struck in the back, clawed the air as if he were trying to escape by climbing the rungs of an invisible ladder. But that wasn't to be. Abruptly he gave a thin, eerie scream, which sent an icy shiver the length of the sniper's back. Next instant, he plunged face-forward on to the body of the man he had just murdered so cold-bloodedly, dead himself. Then there was silence…

'Comrade general,' the aide said cautiously. 'Comrade general, have you a moment for one of the snipers?'

General Chuikov looked up from his paper-littered desk, a scowl on his bejowled, seamed face, and thrust back the lock of tousled, black hair from his forehead. 'In three devils' names, why should I have time for a damned sniper, eh?'

The aide licked his lips nervously. The commander of the Stalingrad defence forces was a difficult man to get along with. His staff feared him more than the Fritzes. This wouldn't be the first or the last time that he had flung an aide out of the window into the debris-littered street. 'It seems that the sniper has some information of importance, general,' he said and swallowed hard.

'*Boshe moi*!' Chuikov cursed and lit a long cigarette with a bandaged hand that covered the weeping eczema which afflicted him, the result of months of nervous strain. 'Bring him in.'

The aide opened his mouth momentarily. 'Yes, comrade general,' he said and went out, leaving Chuikov puffing gloomily at his cigarette, hardly aware of the thunder of the *katuska* rocket guns outside and the stomach-churning howl of the Fritz electric mortars answering them from the other side of the Volga.

'The sniper, comrade general,' the aide announced and indicated the slight figure standing to his rear, muffled in thick, wadded jacket and heavy fur-felt boots, with a spoon stuck down the side of the right one.

'Well?' Chuikov asked grumpily, eyeing the sniper who looked like the rest of his kind, save that this one had an almost boyish cast of features — probably hadn't even started shaving yet. 'What tremendous, world-shaking news have you for me, comrade?'

His cynicism was wasted on the sniper, whose wooden expression did not change. 'This, comrade general.' The sniper placed what looked like a map, stained red with blood, on Chuikov's desk and stepped back smartly.

Gingerly, as if afraid to get his fingers soiled, Chuikov picked up the map and unfolded it with some difficulty; the blood had become as thick as jam between the sheets. He pulled a face.

Expressionlessly, the sniper and the aide waited for Chuikov's reaction.

With a roar, Chuikov smashed his good hand down on the desk. 'By the black virgin of Kazan!' he exclaimed with delight. 'It's a general staff map of the Fritz positions!'

He beamed at the sniper, who now beamed back at him. 'Tell me, little brother,' he said eagerly, 'tell me the details of how you found this map. We must be quite sure that it is not a Fritz plant. They have pulled that sort of trick before.'

Hastily the sniper explained how one Fritz had shot the other before succumbing himself, and how, even in his death throes, the German staff officer had clutched the map to his bleeding body in a vain attempt to blot out the tell-tale red and blue crayon marks with his own blood.

Chuikov's eyes narrowed when the sniper was finished. 'It all rings true,' he said slowly. 'Obviously the big Fritz didn't want the pilot to fall into our hands. He thought he might sing like a canary once our — er — specialists —' he gave the sniper the benefit of his gold toothed smile — 'started to work upon him. It was better to have him dead. Then he would have destroyed the map and probably shot himself. Yes, it all fits into place very nicely… You have done a fine job, comrade.' He turned to the attentive aide. 'Pepper vodka and glasses, the big ones,' he snapped.

Hurriedly, the aide went to the cabinet where the general kept his own special brand of vodka. He produced two water glasses and the bottle. The general took them from his hand and poured the glasses full to the brim. 'Sit down, comrade,' he said, in high good humour now. 'Take off your cap and make yourself comfortable. Today you've had the best bag in your whole shooting career.'

Confused, a little red-faced at being asked to sit in the presence of a general, the sniper took a chair and pulled off his fur cap. Blonde curls cascaded down, released now from the constraints of the cap.

Now it was Chuikov's turn to be confused. 'What … what's your name, comrade?' he stuttered.

'Chernova, Tania,' the sniper answered in a small voice, eyeing the glasses greedily.

'But you're a woman … *a female woman!*' Chuikov stuttered. Then he recovered himself and handed her the water glass full of vodka with a great flourish, once more in control of himself. 'Well, I must say, Chernova, Tania, this is a day of surprises! For you, for me, and now, with this,' he touched the blood-stained map, 'the Fritzes.' He raised his glass in toast. '*Nastrovya, pan!*'

'*Nastrovya, pan!*' she repeated the toast eagerly.

Together, watched by an amazed aide who didn't think that a slip of a girl like this sniper could drink that much, the two of them swallowed the fiery spirits, their cheeks beginning to glow, their eyes sparkling, as they drained it down steadily, until finally Chuikov was finished, followed a second later by the girl.

Tipsy now, Chuikov swayed to his feet. 'Comrade sniper,' he bellowed, 'Death to the fascists! Victory to the Soviet Union!' With all his strength he flung his water glass at the wall, where it shattered into a hundred gleaming shards.

Carried away by the excitement of the moment, the girl did the same, crying, '*Victory at Stalingrad*...!'

BOOK ONE: *STALINGRAD*

CHAPTER 1

'Stalingrad!' Colonel Katukov said simply, reining-in his big grey mare as the group of officers breasted the hill, while the weary infantry of the 333rd Punishment Battalion, known as the 'Gulag rats', toiled up the rest of the steep slope.

Major Boldin, the battalion's second-in-command, gasped. He had fought over two continents ever since he was seventeen, and since the Fritzes had invaded Mother Russia in the summer of the previous year, he had seen more than enough of slaughter and horror; but he had never viewed anything like the scene stretched out below in the curve of the Volga.

The great city was ringed with fire, great orange balloons of flame exploding all the time, while the city itself, hugging the serpentine bends of the Volga like some monstrous caterpillar, belched huge spouts of flame and debris as shell after shell struck home. The noise was ear-splitting; a hideous man-made cacophony that seemed to strike the awed onlookers like a physical blow.

'God in heaven!' the bespectacled Vulf gasped in awe. 'It's how I visualize Dante's hell!'

Colonel Katukov turned round and looked coldly at the pale-faced lieutenant who affected the horn-rimmed glasses of the pre-war university teacher. '*Tovarisch mladshi-leitenant*,' he snapped in that cold, crisp manner of his, his grey eyes piercing Vulf, 'that is not hell! At this moment you are being privileged — and the rest of that gulag scum up there' — he indicated the first weary 'rats', burdened by forty kilos of equipment, who were now breasting the height — 'to catch a glimpse of paradise. That is Stalingrad, a holy place, which has stopped every enemy effort to cross the Volga these last three months or more. Down there the fascist beast is bleeding to death.'

His words ended abruptly as a colossal yellow fireball exploded only fifty metres away, uprooting the snow-heavy firs, snapping them as if they were matchsticks and setting the wood alight immediately.

'Comrade colonel,' Boldin said coldly, while the other officers bent low over their horses' heads, trying to calm the trembling beasts and avoid the red-hot, fist-sized fragments of steel which flew everywhere, scything down anything that came in their way, 'I think we could leave the history of Stalingrad for a safer place, don't you?'

Katukov, as erect in his saddle as if he were reviewing a peacetime parade, gave him one of his grey stares, then nodded his head. 'Company commanders take charge of your companies. Ensure that there is a senior sergeant posted with a machine-gun to the rear of each company.' His harshly handsome face contorted into a bitter sneer and Boldin could see just how he still hated the command that Beria, the head of the Secret Police, had forced on him in the summer of 1941. 'I don't want my jailbirds running away before they have a chance of redeeming their worthless lives by dying for Mother Russia.'

One company commander went red with shame, another looked down, the other two glared back at their CO, naked hate in their eyes for this 'NKVD Greenhat' who had dragged them from Stalin's jails, the notorious Gulag Archipelago, and expected them to die for the dictator who had condemned them to that living hell.

Boldin nodded slightly. The four of them raised their hands to their fur caps in salute.

Katukov did not even seem to see them.

Shrugging their shoulders, the four captains tugged their horses round and began to trot back to their awestricken companies to carry out the CO's orders.

Katukov turned to Boldin and Vulf. 'You two will come with me,' he said, his tone a little warmer now, for although both of them were gulag rats themselves, he had come to rely and trust in them ever since that great battle in defence of Moscow when they had first come together.

'Comrade, can you hear our voice?... We know it. You must hear it! At this dear hour of our lives. Our first thought goes not to our sons, or to our mothers, but to you, dear comrade Stalin...' Desperately the skinny civilian with the dew-drop hanging from his red beak of a nose read out the poem of praise to the Soviet dictator. All the while whistles shrilled, red-faced NCO's bellowed orders and the lines of pale, nervous reinforcements filed down the river bank towards the waiting barges. The NKVD machine-gunners stood ready to mow down the first man attempting to desert.

The three officers of the gulag rats tethered their horses and joined the long line of heavily laden infantry who were about to embark on the nightmare journey across the Volga, the *politruks* everywhere now, attempting to calm them down with ferocious zeal, reading out exhortations to hate the enemy and be brave, distributing pamphlets entitled, 'What a Soldier needs to Know and How to Act in Street-Fighting' that were dropped into the snow. Even the most naive recruit knew that there was a fifty-fifty chance he would never even reach Stalingrad.

Katukov was seemingly unmoved by the chaos and fear all around him. Instead he lectured the other two as they shuffled towards the waiting barges on 'the drill', as he called it. 'We'll land over there,' he snapped, indicating the smoke-covered far bank. 'There is a cluster of moorings behind the Red October and Barrikady Plants, which are pretty safe. However, the Fritzes have a look-out post on Mamaev Hill, up there. They'll spot us, naturally, and let us have the full weight of their artillery.'

'Naturally!' Vulf echoed sarcastically.

But, as always, sarcasm was wasted on Colonel Katukov. 'If we can get by that area, we're relatively safe,' he continued. 'If we're hit, on the other hand, over the side and swim for it.'

Major Boldin smiled wryly. 'A swim in the Volga in November, comrade colonel,' he commented. 'I think I prefer the Fritz artillery... But if we do have to go over the side, colonel, where do we rendezvous afterwards?'

'Yes,' Vulf added, his curiosity overcoming his fear, 'where *are* we going, comrade colonel?' he grunted as one of the *politruks* dug him in the ribs to hurry him along into the barge. 'And what *is* our mission?'

'The rendezvous I can tell you,' Katukov said, as the *politruks* began to pack them in the barge like sheep being led to the slaughter. 'We are to report to General Chuikov's headquarters to the rear of the 284th Division.'

'And the mission?' Boldin urged, as the whistles shrilled and sailors in red-striped shirts and floppy, beribboned caps started to toss the cables on to the shore.

Katukov shrugged. 'That I do not know, *tavorisch major.*'

Vulf, pressed up tight against the back of a squat Siberian infantryman, who stank of rancid butter and black *mahorka* tobacco, shook his head with difficulty. 'Typical,' he said to no one in particular. 'The gulag rats are going to be right down in the shit with their hooters again.'

The barge quivered. Its screws raced furiously. The water churned in a wild white fury. And then they were off. The journey across the Volga had commenced. Next to Boldin, a white-faced youth with curly hair and frightened eyes started to pray. Major Boldin could understand why.

'The fascists have taken every single decency away from you! Everything! Liberty, justice, happiness, truth, the beauty of life itself! Give what you have left. Give your lives if necessary...' The politruk's face strained with the effort, but still he kept a wary finger on the trigger of his pistol.

No one listened. Everyone's gaze was now fixed on the Manaev Hill, which loomed out of the fog of war. There was no doubt that the Fritzes were watching them. But would their observers be able to call up their artillery before they had passed out of sight?

Boldin swung a glance behind him. There were eight or ten barges chugging stoutly in their wake, packed to the gunwales with reinforcements, their frightened mass praying, clearly audible above the thunder of the barrage. He bit his bottom lip. The barges would make a very tempting target for any Fritz artilleryman who knew his stuff. With difficulty, he freed one hand and undid his tight collar. In case he had to make a jump for it, he didn't want to be strangled by the damn thing. Vulf caught the movement and did the same. Boldin flashed him a gleaming smile with his stainless steel teeth and whispered, 'Courage, little brother.'

'Everybody in the battalion knows I'm a devout coward,' he answered with an attempt at bravery and tucked away his precious horn-rimmed spectacles.

Now as they came ever closer to the danger point, the whole group of *politruks* positioned around the rails to prevent anyone jumping overboard prematurely, broke into a fervent chant, like monks babbling their prayers, their eyes wide and wild with fear too. '*Into battle for our holy homeland... Love of country is stronger than death ... The officer's order is the soldier's law of iron...*'

There was a great rending, tearing sound which drowned the chant.

'*Fritz eighty-eight!*' someone screamed wildly.

Fifty metres away, the hundred-pound shell struck the water. The river erupted. Water drenched them and the barge rocked wildly as if struck by a sudden tornado.

That single shell seemed to act as a signal. In an instant the air above the Volga was filled with flying steel. Flame spurted everywhere. Great balls of orange fire started to explode among the barges, whipping the water into a wild, white fury, sending the craft reeling crazily from side to side. The first barge was hit. A body hurtled through the smoke and smashed against the leading craft to burst like a ripe melon. Abruptly the boiling water was full of screaming, drowning men.

Boldin jammed his elbow into the back of the man in front of him so that he would make room. Hastily he pulled off his boots and slung them around his neck. Katukov, his face now grim, hesitated only a minute and then as the obscene, stomach-churning whine of the German multiple mortars began to fill the air, he did the same. The reinforcements began to panic. Here and there a pistol cracked as a crazed soldier attempted to go over the side. Hoarsely the *politruks* cried above the tremendous racket, 'Stand firm, comrades, for God's sake, stand firm!'

Another barge took a direct hit. It broke in half immediately and went down like a stone, bearing its cargo of dead men with it, leaving a solitary soldier on the surface trying desperately to swim after the lead barge, although both his legs had been severed. His cry for help ended in a gurgle of water as he went under.

A German phosphorus shell landed on the barge directly behind theirs. It exploded in a burst of blinding, incandescent flame. Like a great roaring blowtorch, it hissed the length of the barge, ripping the flesh off the trapped soldiers, turning them into hunched, blackened pygmies in an instant, leaving the craft to zigzag wildly about the Volga with its cargo, completely out of control.

Major Boldin had had enough. He grabbed Katukov by the shoulder. 'Katukov, it's over the side!' he yelled above the howl and whine of the German shells.

'But the example,' Katukov began to protest, no fear in those cold, grey eyes of his.

Boldin cut him short with an angry snort. 'Damn the example!' he roared and ducked as their barge heeled under the impact of several tons of water smashing into its side. 'It's only a matter of seconds before they hit us. I don't want to be slaughtered purposelessly like a sheep in a pen! Are you coming?'

'*Horoscho*, I come!'

'After me, Vulf,' Boldin commanded and shoved his way forward.

The civilian with the red dripping nose drew his pistol, his eyes a mixture of fear and contempt. 'Ah, the gulag rats are the first to leave the sinking ship, eh? What else can one expect from treacherous scum like you? I —'

With all his strength, Boldin jammed his elbow into the man's skinny face. Something snapped. The civilian screamed thinly and went reeling over the side to hit the foaming water with a splash.

'Report me to Old Leather Face, you shitty civilian!' he cried contemptuously and dived neatly over the side the next instant.

Vulf followed, then Katukov. Treading water, Boldin waited, then cried, in complete charge of the situation now, 'Right, after me! Keep together. Anyone tries to grab you in the water, smack him under the nose with the palm of your hand. *Davoi!*'

Swimming strongly, his big, almost brutal shoulder-muscles rippling under the material of his tunic, he struck out for the shore, leaving the barge to sail on to its inevitable destruction. Gasping, spluttering, spitting out river water, and shaking with the cold, the three of them squatted on the sand bank, the river behind shrouded with burning smoke through which came the awful screams and pathetic cries for help of the wounded and the drowning.

Carefully Vulf put on his precious horn-rims and peered owlishly at the muddy bank which loomed up some twenty metres away. 'What now?' he asked.

Boldin looked at Katukov, who frowned but said nothing. Boldin forced a smile, in spite of the icy cold. 'We might be within our own lines and we might be in theirs. But either way, it's no good sitting here. Another five minutes and we'll be frozen solid.'

'Agreed,' Katukov said and loosening the pistol in his holster began to walk to the edge of the water. They followed and started to wade cautiously through the shallows towards the bank.

There Katukov halted. 'I'll go first,' he ordered. 'Who knows what our people might make of you two.' He drew his pistol and indicated their uniforms which, like those of the other gulag rats, were devoid of badges of rank and unit insignia.

Vulf forced a grin. 'Agreed, comrade colonel. It's hardly likely that our own boys would shoot a Greenhat — at least not from the front!'

Katukov glared at him and began to clamber up the bank while they crouched there, dripping water and shivering, weapons at the ready.

Five minutes later Katukov was slithering down towards them once more, his face grim, and Boldin knew without his saying that they had come ashore in German territory. 'Fritzes?' he whispered.

Katukov nodded. 'Yes, there seems to be a heavy artillery battery up there. Can't make them out clearly in this damned smoke. But they're Fritzes all right.'

Vulf looked at Boldin, but said nothing. Boldin knew what the little intellectual was thinking. If the two of them fell into German hands, they would get the usual kicks and blows, but that would be it. The Fritzes would send them back to the POW cages. With Katukov and his damned green-cross cap badge, it would be different. The Fritzes always shot NKVD men and they might well shoot them, too.

Katukov made his decision. 'We'll bluff it out. In the smoke they'll not be able to make out our uniforms clearly. If they do, we'll make a run for it.'

Boldin nodded his agreement and Vulf frowned. In spite of the treatment Boldin had received from the NKVD in the gulag and the fact that they had helped to destroy his whole life, his military career, even his marriage — for his wife had committed suicide after his arrest, and his boy had vanished into one of the Stalin scholar schools — he couldn't betray his commanding officer. Boldin the gulag rat would lay down his life for the stern-faced NKVD colonel if called upon to do so.

Stealing up the steep bank as quietly as they could, the three of them crouched there momentarily, eyeing the Fritzes through the drifting smoke as they fed shell after shell into their howitzers. The slight wind brought snatches of commands in German towards them and every fresh explosion slapped them in the face with a hot wave of acrid burnt air until Katukov commanded in a whisper, 'Come on. This way!'

Time passed leadenly as they worked their way along the river bank, their slow progress punctuated by the regular thump-thump of heavy guns and the high-pitched whirr of German machine-guns sending red tracer hissing across the river like angry hornets. At another time those Spandau's would have drawn the three men's curses, but not now. That distinctive, frenzied, hysterical sound told them that they were still within German-held territory. Now they began to creep through German outposts. Time and time again they froze at the occasional German voice or the sudden flare hissing into the grey-smoke sky to hang there for what seemed an eternity, bathing everything below in its eerie, unreal light.

Creeping behind Boldin, pistol held in a hand that shook badly, Vulf whispered, 'For God's sake, comrade major, how much longer? I can already feel the stuff trickling down into my right boot!'

Boldin grinned. Vulf was a card. 'Not much, little brother.'

In the front, Katukov hissed sternly, 'Be quiet, the two of you. Listen!'

Katukov cocked his head to one side and the others did the same. A well-remembered sound was coming from somewhere to their right. There was no mistaking the slow metallic chatter like that of an irate ancient woodpecker. It was the Red Army '05 model machine-gun all right.

'Our lines, colonel?' Boldin queried.

'Right, comrade major,' Katukov answered, advancing again, body bent as if against a strong wind, pistol at the ready, face tense. Boldin knew why. This would be the most dangerous stage of their little adventure. Front-line soldiers were notoriously trigger-happy. Even if they did manage to break through the Fritz lines, they would still have to contend with their own people out there somewhere. In this chaos, with vision reduced by the smoke and fog to about ten metres, the infantry might well shoot first and ask questions afterwards.

Carefully, they started to skirt a collection of ruined apartment houses, working their way to the sound of that old-fashioned machine-gun. To their left a Russian direct hit ripped the fog of war apart with dramatic, electric suddenness and they glimpsed pieces of metal or body flying into the air. A horse slammed into the ground directly in front of them, followed by a barbed-wire entanglement, its posts still attached to it, so that it looked like a huge net flung by some sea-giant to entrap them. Vulf gulped audibly and stepped over the carcass of the dead horse. '*Boshe moi!*' he said in a little voice, 'What in the name of all that is holy will come down next?'

Now they could catch fragmentary glances of their own positions between the gaps in the house walls before they disappeared again in the smoke which billowed up like foam: a lunar landscape of churned-up brown craters against the white of the snow, rent apart time and time again by rust-red spurts of angry flame. It looked to Vulf like the end of the world. Wordlessly, they started to mount the stairs of an intact stairwell, knowing that they might well be able to get to the other side through the second floor without being seen by the

Fritzes dug in around the building. On tip-toe, like children out to play some prank on their unsuspecting fellows, they crept up the stairs, their hearts beating like triphammers now, their hands, gripping their pistols, wet with sweat.

'*Hände hoch*!' The challenge cut into Vulf s back like a knife. He swung round.

A big German stood there, eyes blood-shot under his helmet, heavy, pugnacious chin covered with stubble, rifle in hand.

Instinctively Vulf lashed out with his foot. The German howled with pain. His rifle dropped from his nerveless fingers and clattered to the floor while he reeled against the wall.

Boldin's pistol cracked. The German was swung round by the impact at such short range. He fell screaming over the rail to slam to the floor below like a sack of wet cement.

'*Davoi*!' Katukov yelled, knowing now that it was no use attempting to conceal their presence in the house as cries of rage and alarm shot up on all sides. They had stumbled into a hornet's nest of enemy soldiers.

A German tried to bar Boldin's escape. Boldin smashed his pistol against the man's face. Blood shot from the soldier's smashed nose. He went down howling with agony. Boldin slammed his heavy boot into the man's contorted face and ran on. Two Germans sprang out of a side room, firing their rifles from the hip as they came. Slugs howled off the walls. Plaster trickled down on the Russian fugitives like grey snow. Katukov snapped off a shot to left and right. Both men went down, as if pole-axed.

Boldin stumbled on a loose plank and nearly fell. It saved his life. To his right, a bare-headed Fritz with a machine-pistol clasped to his hip, ripped off an angry burst. The slugs stitched a smoking line of holes just above his head. Behind the major, Vulf pressed his trigger. The bullet caught the German squarely in the chest. He slapped back against the wall, as if propelled there by a gigantic fist.

To their front now lay a large shattered window. Through it, Katukov in the lead could see the red flag with its dearly loved hammer and sickle, waving weakly in the faint breeze. It was the Red Army's line. 'This way,' he gasped and bolted forward, head tucked between his shoulders like a footballer, ignoring the wild shots which whined off the walls on all sides, pocking the plaster with ugly little spurts of blue flame.

Boldin and Vulf rushed after him. Boldin felt a dozen bullets tug at his uniform and the sudden, passing heat on his face as they cut the air close to his cheeks. Still he ran with the last of his strength, gasping leathern-lunged like an ancient bellows, knowing that it was now or never. If they didn't escape through that window, the Fritzes would trap them.

Katukov hesitated only momentarily, then, with a great roar, a compound of rage, fear and anger, he went through. Vulf hesitated.

'Jump, you little shit!' Boldin cried in anger. He lifted his boot and levelled a great kick at Vulf's baggy breeches. He flew through the window to slam down hard on the brick rubble fifteen metres below, followed by Boldin. And then the three of them, bruised and bleeding, were up and running for their very lives towards their own positions, cheered on by the Red Army men standing up in their trenches now, waving their helmets like excited spectators at some sports contest, followed by the frustrated fire of the Fritzes, cheated of their prey this one time. They had done it. They were now in Stalingrad!

CHAPTER 2

The Red Army's engineers had blasted a T-shaped tunnel on the cliff side of the west bank of the Volga to the rear of the 284th Infantry Division, boring twenty metres below the surface to make the tunnel safe against anything but a direct hit with a heavy-calibre shell. This was General Chuikov's fourth headquarters in the seven weeks he had commanded the army defending Stalingrad.

Now, drinking hot tea laced with vodka, warming their frozen hands on the glasses, Major Boldin and Lieutenant Vulf waited outside in the dirty snow, watching the hectic traffic in and out of the tunnel while Colonel Katukov sought an interview with the army commander.

In spite of the languid, apparently bored manner of the elegant, pale-faced staff officers grouped at the entrance, catching a breath of air and smoking their cigarettes in holders, little Vulf could see that all was not well in Stalingrad. The couriers who kept appearing from the front were mud-stained, their uniforms ragged, sometimes red with blood, as if they had been forced to run the gauntlet of enemy fire to reach the HQ. And their eyes revealed everything — they were wide and wild, the eyes of men who were plain scared.

Vulf pressed the last few drops of precious lemon juice into his tea and said softly, so that the staff officers at the entrance couldn't hear him, 'The situation at Stalingrad doesn't look particularly healthy, Boldin. I think General Chuikov has problems.'

Boldin nodded his agreement, taking his gaze off the pitiful line of wounded filing past the tunnel, some of them barefoot in the snow, all of them terribly emaciated, with the blinded men bringing up the rear, hanging on to each other's belts helplessly. 'Yes, you're right, Vulf, Vassili Chuikov looks to me as if he's in a fix here.'

'And thousands die for a matter of prestige,' Vulf sneered. 'On the one side, the German dictator Hitler wants to capture the city because it bears the name of his hated rival Stalin, and on the other, Old Leather Face must defend it to the end so that *his* Stalingrad does not fall into Fritz's hand. Because of that, all Russia bleeds.' He spat contemptuously into the snow.

'What treacherous thoughts,' Boldin said mildly. 'It would be back to the gulag or worse for you if the NKVD heard you spouting such disloyal sentiments about our beloved leader.'

'I shit on the NKVD!' Vulf grunted and spat again.

Boldin smiled slightly at the little man's outraged look. 'You know, little brother, if fate had had it otherwise, I might well have been in command here this day instead of Vassili Chuikov.'

'What do you mean?' Vulf looked up curiously at the big major with the bold eyes and handsome face, marred only by a slight, bitter droop of the lips which indicated a disappointed man.

'Chuikov was my second-in-command in the Far East that year when the NKVD arrested me and dragged me off to the gulag.' He paused suddenly and remembered once again that nightmare march to the camps, the new prisoners dying by the score, urged on by the Siberians on their ponies, their bull-penis whips flaying the backs of those still able to march. 'Yes, he was fortunate enough to be sent off to Chungking soon afterwards to report on the Chinese. He escaped the Red Army purges that way. Besides,' he smiled softly, 'the good Vassili is a true proletarian. A peasant and a communist who commanded a regiment at the age of twenty-five in the Civil War. He has all the right qualifications for a Soviet hero. Still,' Boldin paused momentarily, 'if I had been sent to China to watch the Chinese instead of Vassili, who knows who might be commanding in Stalingrad today?'

Vulf touched the big major's arm softly. 'The past, Boldin, the past,' he whispered. 'Besides, thank God you are not in command. Look at that!'

He indicated the tall figure of a young colonel staggering towards the entrance of the tunnel like a drunken man, leaving a trail of blood behind him on the snow, croaking, 'My regiment's gone … gone…'

Hastily the group of staff officers grabbed hold of him by the arm and forced the hysterical officer to sit down in the snow, while they summoned the sentries to take him away. General Chuikov could not be troubled by such hysterics.

The sentries led the colonel away, still croaking 'My regiment's gone'. If he was lucky, they'd take him to the nearest field hospital; if he was unlucky, it would be a quick bullet at the back of the head in the shelter of some wrecked building.

'Poor bastard,' Boldin said and then straightened up. Colonel Katukov was striding across the snow in a great hurry.

'Hello, where's the fire?' Vulf whispered, hastily swallowing the last of his tea.

'We'll soon find out.'

Some twenty metres away from them, the big colonel halted and waved. '*Davoi*!' he called, 'General Chuikov will see us. He's given us fifteen minutes!' He emphasized the time as if they were being granted a great honour. 'Come!' Imperiously he turned and strode towards the entrance of the tunnel HQ.

Vulf shook his head in mock wonder. 'Crap said the king and a thousand arseholes bent and took the strain, for in those days the word of the king was law,' he sneered, but dutifully enough he followed his big friend in the colonel's wake.

Chuikov rose from behind his desk, his blouse so unkempt and devoid of decorations that he might well have been taken for a common soldier, and extended his unbandaged hand to Katukov. 'Welcome, comrade colonel. I am glad to see you here in Stalingrad.' They shook hands and Katukov, his face flushed with pride at his reception by the man who was a triple Hero of the Soviet Union, turned and said, 'My officers, Major Boldin, my second-in-command, and Second Lieutenant Vulf, the battalion intelligence officer.

Chuikov thrust out his hand. 'Comrade marshal' he gasped, mouth dropping open stupidly, hand suddenly suspended in mid-air. 'Why…?'

'No, comrade general,' Boldin said tonelessly, his face revealing nothing, though inwardly he was enjoying the look of absolute surprise on his former second-in-command's face. 'No longer marshal, just a simple major of infantry — and a gulag rat to boot.'

'*Da, da, ya* ponemayu' Chuikov stuttered, recovering his pose, 'I understand.' He indicated to his aide to bring glasses and vodka. 'Sit down, the three of you,' he ordered.

Mildly amused, Boldin did so with the rest, noting that even one of the most powerful men in the Red Army dare not be seen shaking the hand of a gulag rat — they were indeed the outcasts of the Soviet Republic.

Chuikov waited until the aide had poured the glasses full of the fiery spirit, then dismissed him with the command, 'Fifteen minutes. Then you're back. Understood?'

'Understood, comrade general.'

Immediately the usual toasts were over, Chuikov got down to business, undisturbed by the fact that the sirens were sounding their shrill warning that the German dive-bombers were on their way once again. 'Comrades, our position here in Stalingrad is intolerable … but not impossible. The hand-to-hand fighting for the factory has consumed battalions, regiments, even whole divisions of my 62nd Army including Gurtiev's 308th Infantry division.' He looked sharply at Boldin.

Instinctively Boldin nodded in response to that look; he knew General Gurtiev. They had studied together at the Frunze Military Academy.

The whole division was massacred at the battle for the Barrikady. They went in eight thousand strong and came out with two hundred and fifty survivors.' The pugnacious general stopped for a moment and allowed the information to sink in.

Outside the Stukas hurtled from the sky above Stalingrad, their sirens howling hideously. Everywhere in the Soviet-held part of the shattered city the flak guns started to bark.

'Not only that, comrades, but reinforcements and supplies are terribly difficult to get through by day, as you know yourselves — to your cost.' He indicated their damp, muddy uniforms. 'Now my observers tell me that ice sludge is beginning to drift into the Volga, so that until the ice stops moving and forms a solid bridge there will be difficulty in bringing supplies and troops across even at night when those damned Fritz artillerymen on the hill can't spot the barges.' He sighed and added, 'Intolerable, comrades, but not *impossible*, as I have already said.' He took the bottle and refilled their glasses with the pepper vodka.

A moment or two passed while his guests placed salt in the web of skin formed by stretching out their forefingers and thumbs, licking it, and then downing the fiery spirit to the accompaniment of gasps and coughs.

Chuikov wiped his lips with his bandaged hand and Boldin caught a glimpse of the scabs and lesions which ran the length of his forearm. He realized that Vassili must be under tremendous strain in spite of his outspoken, abrasive manner.

'So, comrades, that's the bad news,' Chuikov continued, his eyes sparkling with the drink now. 'This is the good. Yesterday Comrade Stalin informed me that the Red Army will commence its great offensive to beat the Fritzes on the Stalingrad front at zero six-thirty hours on the morning of November nineteenth exactly two weeks from now.'

Katukov gave a little gasp and even Vulf looked impressed.

Chuikov chuckled, obviously pleased with the effect of his surprise. 'Yes, comrades, Operation Uranus, as the attack is code-named, will sweep the Fritzes from the Volga and set them off running to their own accursed homeland for good.' He reached into his desk drawer and pulled out a blood-stained map. 'This,' he announced, spreading it out on the desk in front of them, 'was taken from the body of a German staff officer last week by one of our girl snipers.' He winked suddenly. 'A very pretty one, too.'

Colonel Katukov frowned and Vulf told himself that the NKVD man was a puritan. He had been forced to accept the vodka because the army commander himself had offered him it, but he didn't like strong drink. Nor did he like the reference to the woman.

'We are absolutely certain that it is not a plant. Intelligence confirms much of the detail it contains. Now, look here, we have the German Sixth Army under von Paulus around to the west of Stalingrad, in this natural land bridge between the rivers Don and Volga.' He swept his bandaged hand across the map, criss-crossed with a rash of blue and red crayon marks. 'In this area he has concentrated practically all his combat divisions for the purpose of capturing the city. Clear?'

'Clear,' they answered in unison, voices firm and decisive, though all three of them were wondering why Chuikov had revealed the details of the top-secret offensive to them. What had all this got to do with the gulag rats?

'Now von Paulus has stationed most of his supply dumps needed to feed, clothe and arm those divisions on the far side of the Don to the west where it makes that large loop before curving southwards to the Sea of Azov.'

He pointed to the area with his forefinger.

Outside there was the thud and crump of the Stukas' 250-pound bombs landing all around the entrance to the tunnel. But the general did not seem to notice as he studied the map, ignoring the concrete dust drifting down like thin snow on his bowed shoulders.

'As is, of course, clear to you, comrades, cut von Paulus off from those supplies and his vaunted Sixth Army will wither away just like that!' he snapped his fingers contemptuously. 'Add to that cutting-off of his supplies another thrust from the south, and von Paulus is trapped. Sooner or later he and his three hundred thousand soldiers will surrender and tamely march into the POW cages.'

A bomb landed close by and the bunker shook violently under its impact.

'Three hundred thousand soldiers!' Chuikov repeated the figure, obviously undisturbed by the near miss.

Even Vulf, a born sceptic, was impressed. With German troops virtually at the door of his HQ, half his army dead or wounded, his own headquarters under aerial attack, the tousled-haired general talked of tremendous victories; it was some performance.

'Now then, comrades, Party Secretary Comrade Stalin has ordered that the first priority of Operation Uranus is to cut the Fritzes off from those supplies, then the pincer movement will follow. But comrades, where should that particular thrust take place? I can tell you that it is easier to pinpoint where the two pincers should link up. Here at the bridge across the Don near Kalach.'

Boldin and Katukov nodded their heads in agreement. The only bridge across the Don in the whole area was the most obvious place. They could see, too, the reason why Chuikov found it difficult to make a decision about where the attack on the supplies should start. The Don was simply too full of curves and bends where a determined enemy could hold out or even launch a counter-attack across the river into the Russian flank.

'However, this captured map,' Chuikov continued, 'has helped us to make our decision where we should jump off. According to it, most of that area is held by Dumitrescu's Third Romanian Army. From what we know of them they are poorly led, poorly armed, the Fritzes regard them as more of a burden than anything else, and the rank-and-file have no stomach to fight for that decadent, skirt-chasing king of theirs. Obviously the Romanians are the weak link. So it has been decided that our attack on November nineteenth should be launched across the Don between Serafimovich and Kletskaya — here and here.' He held up a finger in warning. 'However, can we be sure that there are only Romanians in the area? We have lost the Fritz General Heim's Forty-eighth Panzer Corps, an elite formation, and although our Fifth and Twenty-first Tank Armies which will spearhead the attack are good formations, they are no match for Heim's tankers.' He paused and let his words sink in.

From outside there came the sound of muffled cheering. Obviously the gunners protecting the tunnel HQ had brought down one of the gull-winged dive-bombers.

'It is therefore imperative comrades, that we know *now* if it is only the Romanians who bar the way for us on our drive to Kalach.' He looked from one face to the other. 'It will be the task of the 333rd Punishment Battalion to find that out.'

As if he had been listening behind the door waiting for exactly this moment of shocked silence, the elegant aide appeared and, springing to attention, bellowed at the top of his thin voice, 'As commanded, I take the liberty of reminding the comrade army commander that fifteen minutes precisely have passed.'

Chuikov rose to his feet.

The three officers did the same.

'You will be supplied with German uniforms,' Chuikov said, giving them no time to recover from their shock. 'You will cross the River Don tomorrow night. It has all been arranged. You will reconnoitre the area as described and you will report directly to me.' He touched his bandaged hand to his dark, curly hair. 'Comrades, you are dismissed.' He slumped down at his desk and immediately began working on his papers.

Numbly, the three gulag rats allowed themselves to be led outside by the elegant aide, blinking in the sudden grey light, like sheep being led to slaughter.

It was only when the aide had left them with the information that the general's personal launch would take them back across the river that Vulf cried, 'But in the name of all that's holy, do you know what the Fritzes will do if they catch us in their uniforms?' His eyes, desperate and wild, flashed to the sky, as if he were appealing to God himself.

'Yes,' said Katukov in a voice drained of emotion. 'They'll shoot us.'

CHAPTER 3

The giant oaks trenched the darkening skyline like the teeth of an upturned rake. The opposite bank of the River Don lay still and apparently empty. Admittedly the peasants and *kolhoz* farmers had fled long ago, but there were men over there all right, frightened, desperate, savage men — just as the watchers crouched in the snow were frightened, desperate and savage.

'This is the narrowest stretch of the Don,' their young guide, a former collective farmer from the other side, now a volunteer for the Red Army, told them.

Behind them, the dogs made uneasy by the whisper of the wind in the oaks started to bark and howl at the silver crescent of the moon which cast its spectral light on the gulag rats crouched everywhere in the reeds and snow. 'Quieten those damned hounds!' Katukov snapped angrily. 'At once!'

Vulf doubled away to carry out the order. The officers resumed their study of the opposite bank.

'If you would care to focus your glasses at ten o'clock, comrade colonel,' the ex-farmer said in that slow, polite manner of the Don people, 'you'll see one of their outposts covering the tunnel.'

Katukov and Boldin did so and the tall helmets of the Romanian Army came into focus.

'They'll be little problem once we're across,' Katukov grunted. Behind them, the howling of the special dogs had ceased. Boldin told himself that for a city man, Vulf had a way with animals. He actually seemed to like the half-wild Alsatians which were going to cross the river with them.

'At two o'clock, comrade colonel,' the boy said hesitantly, 'they've got some armour — next to that ruined barn.'

Obediently, the two officers swung their night glasses round. A handful of light tanks, outlined in stark black against the faint silver light, swung into view.

'Hmm,' Boldin commented, 'I doubt if they're going to be able to start them easily in this cold — it's freezing the eggs off me!' He shivered dramatically. 'But if their cannon are manned, they certainly could make goulash out of the battalion emerging from the tunnel in dribs and drabs.'

'Agreed,' Katukov said, lowering his binoculars. For a few minutes he appeared sunk in thought, wreathed in a gloomy silence, while the rest waited for his decision. Across the river a red flare hissed into the sky. It hung there, bathing the gulag rats who had frozen into immobility in its unreal, glowing blood-red light. They tensed, waiting for the first snarl of a machine-gun, but none came. They had not been spotted. The Romanians were nervous; the flares were just a routine measure. The flare dropped to the water and died with a small hiss, leaving them blinking their eyes in the sudden inky darkness.

'We'll do it like this,' Katukov said. 'Boldin, you take the lead assault party. In that uniform, you might fool the Rumanian outposts long enough to be able to deal with them before they start firing and waking up the whole damned Third Romanian Army.'

Boldin, in an ill-fitting German major's uniform, nodded his agreement. 'I'll do my best, comrade colonel.'

'Then I'll follow with Vulf and the dogs. I'll head straight for those light tanks. If I fail to capture them, we'll have to use the dogs…' He turned to the ex-farmer. 'All right, comrade,' he snapped, 'let's be on our way.'

'Yes, comrade colonel … and comrade colonel?'

'Yes?'

'Can I go with Major Boldin's party?' the boy drew a long, wicked-looking knife from the side of his boot, his innocent child's face suddenly contorted into a wolfish grimace, dark eyes blazing with hate. 'I have a score to settle with those Romanian swine.'

'Yes, little brother, you can go with Comrade Boldin.' He laid an almost fatherly hand on the boy's shoulder. 'But don't do anything foolish and dangerous. Mother Russia will have need of you and your kind in the years after this terrible war.'

Boldin shook his head in mock wonder. Was the harsh-faced NKVD man a sentimentalist at heart after all? Then they were gone, stealing into the silver gloom like grey timber wolves intent on their prey.

The stench of the tunnel underneath the Don hit Katukov an almost physical blow in the face. He blanched and hesitated. '*Boshe moi*,' he cursed thickly. 'What an evil stench.'

The guide smiled and stepped forward, hissing carbide lantern held up at the ready. 'It is two hundred years old, comrade colonel. They say that Stenka Razin, the Cossack leader, had it built, on his way to take Stalingrad.'

'Hmm,' Katukov grunted, tying a handkerchief round his mouth and nose, 'it smells like it.' He indicated with a nod of his head that the guide should enter, then turned to Boldin. 'Off you go, comrade. Try to get through their positions with the least possible noise.'

'I will, comrade colonel,' Boldin answered, telling himself that he'd need the devil's own luck to be able to do that.

Time passed incredibly slowly. There was no sound save the drip-drip of the water from the ancient stone roof, the pad-pad of the dogs behind them, and the occasional scurry of clawed feet as the rats, their shadows magnified frighteningly on the walls by the flickering light of the lantern, scurried for safety at their approach.

Boldin, unimaginative soldier that he was, felt uneasy and not a little scared at the thought that he was deep below the Don in this ancient tunnel — what if the roof gave way? — and to take his mind off his fears, he talked to the boy who was leading them. 'What kind of men are these Romanians, little brother? I know nothing of them.'

'Pigs!' the boy snarled and then relented a little. 'Their officers treat them like dirt, comrade major. They're all corseted, perfumed fools who strike their soldiers for the slightest thing, and in their turn the soldiers take it out on us. I understand, but I also hate.'

Their guide's eyes blazed with fury and Boldin shook his head a little sadly. This damned war, he told himself, was turning the average Russian soldier into a ruthless, heartless killer. God knows how such people would ever find their way back to a normal quiet life once there was peace again. *Peace*, said a sudden little cynical voice from the deeper regions of his mind. What kind of peace can you expect, Major Boldin? For you and the rest of the scum, pimps, parasites, politicos who make up the 333rd Punishment Battalion, peace will mean only one thing — providing you manage to survive the war, which is hardly likely — back to the camps!

'Comrade major,' the boy's excited voice cut into his gloomy reverie.

'Yes?'

'Up there ... that's the exit.' He held his lantern a little higher so that Boldin could see the dark, shrub-fringed hole that lay some twenty metres ahead.

'*Horoscho!*' Boldin snapped, everything forgotten now. 'Douse the light, boy.'

Hastily the youth did so and, depositing the lantern on the floor, reached for the long knife tucked down the side of his boot.

'Listen,' Boldin hissed to the men clad in field-grey all around him, 'make as little noise as you can. I aim to get close enough to the Romanians' first position to use our knives.'

'Yes,' the boy whispered eagerly, 'cold steel —'

'Shut up!' Boldin interrupted him brutally. 'All right, follow me and I'll sabre the eggs off any man who gives our position away!'

They emerged into the silver gloom, strung well out, each of the rats clasping a knife, bayonet, or assault-spade, its edges ground until they were razor-sharp. Hardly daring to breathe, they began to work their way towards the first Romanian position. They passed through a copse of snow-heavy firs, moving each frond carefully with their hands in order not to dislodge the snow resting on it. Boldin paused momentarily to take his bearings, sniffing the air like a wild dog, sensing the faint odour of garlic, stale sweat and black tobacco which indicated the presence of men to his right.

Like predatory animals stalking their prey, they crept towards the unsuspecting Romanians, chatting softly with one another in the lazy manner of sentries all over the world, who knew they had a great deal of time to kill. *Fifty metres … thirty metres … twenty-five … twenty … fifteen…* Ever closer…

At ten metres, Boldin indicated that his force should break into two groups. He would take the first group to swing round behind the enemy position; a senior sergeant would advance directly towards it.

They set off once more, bent double, hardly daring to breathe, their hands gripping their weapons wet with sweat. *Five metres to go!* Boldin, his brow lathered in greasy sweat in spite of the night cold, could see the Romanians' outlines quite clearly as they stood with their backs resting against the sandbags, unaware that their last moments on this earth were rapidly drawing near. He drew a deep breath and tried to calm the fluttering of his heart. He was getting too old for this sort of thing, he told himself.

Still the Rumanians continued to chatter softly in their melodious-sounding language, so soft and feminine. *Four metres to go!* In another instant, he would be able to reach out and grab the first soldier by the throat and silence any cry of alarm he might attempt to make. *Three metres!* Boldin tensed for the final dash forward.

Then it happened. Behind him the boy stumbled on a rock jutting up above the surface of the snow. The chatter ceased. The Romanians swung round, machine-pistols and rifles at the ready, faces contorted with fear in the silver gloom as they spotted the intent figures advancing towards them. Boldin knew that it would be no use attempting to bluff them. They would shoot first and ask questions afterwards.

'*Davoi!*' he cried and dived forward.

Scarlet flame split the gloom. Next to him the boy screamed shrilly. The knife clattered from his fingers and he fell face forward into the snow, dead.

The rats streamed forward, screaming, knives, bayonets and spades gleaming in the moonlight, and flung themselves at the surprised Romanians. In a crazy confusion, Russian and Romanian tumbled to the ground, grunting obscenely like wild animals, even fear forgotten now.

A tall soldier who stank of garlic swung his rifle butt at Boldin. The major dodged just in time. His knife flashed wickedly the next second and the Romanian went down, blood seeping through the fingers tightly clutched to his ripped-open throat. Boldin sprang over his writhing body. Another Romanian had thrown down his weapon and was clambering over the parapet in a desperate attempt to escape these blood-crazed killers who had appeared so startlingly out of the night. Boldin's big hand fell on the Romanian's shoulder and heaved. The Romanian lashed back with his elbow. Boldin gasped hard as it connected with his stomach.

The knife fell from his fingers with the shock. Again the Romanian attempted to clamber over the sandbags and escape. Desperately, Boldin, almost doubled up and gasping for breath, grabbed at his foot. The Romanian came tumbling down on to him. Together they fell to the ground in a confused melee, smashing their fists at each other, savagely attempting to gouge one another's eyes out. Boldin's fingers sought and found the writhing Romanian's neck. He grabbed and held. The Romanian's spine arched like a taut bow-string, strange gurgling cries coming from his throat as he writhed and twisted, attempting to break that brutal grip. Boldin held on, feeling the Romanian growing weaker by the moment '*Die, you bastard*!' he grunted fiercely through gritted teeth, knowing he couldn't stand the strain much longer.

'*Die!*'

As if in response, the man's body went limp and Boldin staggered groggily to his feet. He heard, only vaguely, the thin asthmatic whine of an engine being started with difficulty in the freezing night air.

At the exit to the tunnel, Katukov heard that first desperate whine clearly enough. 'Get the damned dogs, Vulf!' he bellowed as one of the tank machine-gunners opened up and sent a wild burst of red and white tracer hissing in their general direction.

'The hounds — quick!'

The dog-handlers didn't wait for Vulf's command. Instantly they slipped off the chains. The heavily laden Alsatians darted forward across the snow as they had been trained to do, hurtling onwards, barking ferociously, ears pricked back, tails low as they ran to their deaths.

The machine-gunner spotted the dark shadows racing across the surface of the snow. Instinctively he knew they meant him no good. He ripped off a hasty salvo in their direction. Dog after dog went down howling pitifully and Vulf thrust his hands to his ears to drown out that terrible sound. But the others raced on and Vulf watched with horrified fascination, as the leading Alsatian squirmed its way underneath the tank.

The prong projecting from the heavy pack-mine on its back triggered off the charge immediately. The tank reeled back on its rear bogies in a thick crump of bright flame like a wild horse being put to the saddle for the first time. Sickened, his throat full of hot vomit, Vulf saw the dog sail through the glare and vanish.

Just behind, the frightened driver of the next tank pressed his foot down hard on the accelerator. The engine roared into violent life. He slammed the gear into reverse, smashing through a little straw *isba* behind him, careening off a third tank that wouldn't start, while its gunner swung the turret round, spitting fire from the m.g. at the half-wild hounds which were everywhere.

Dog after dog rolled over, yelping pitifully, but still the rest came on. Vulf hid his eyes. He could look no longer on this sickening dog-hunt.

Five minutes later it was all over. The dog-handlers were filing slowly back into the tunnel with the survivors, while in the snow the bodies of the dead, so cruelly massacred, both man and animal, started to stiffen rapidly in the night cold.

Vulf gulped hard and tried not to look at the dogs sprawled in the snow in front of the burning tanks. 'Boldin,' he said, 'they are like the gulag rats — animals to be slaughtered at the command of that monster in the Kremlin, cannon-fodder both of us, powerless to determine our own fate.'

Boldin pulled out his precious flask of vodka. 'Here, little brother, drink,' he commanded. 'It is not wise, just now, to think of such things. There will be another time one day and things will change.' But even as he uttered the words of comfort to his old comrade, he knew he was lying. There would never be any change in Russia. Their fate had already been sealed.

A moment later they had gone, stealing into the shadows…

CHAPTER 4

The 333rd Punishment Battalion was not the only unit engaged in clandestine operations that cold November night. Some fifty kilometres away in the ruins of embattled Stalingrad, a small group of soldiers in the field-grey of the Wehrmacht were also conducting an armed reconnaissance into no-man's land, the home of deserters and criminals, and the snipers of both armies.

Every man of the volunteer force knew that even at night the Red Army posted snipers among the grotesque mess of tangled steel and shattered brickwork that had once been a prosperous workers' settlement. Cautiously, they advanced to the site of the wreck which had been pinpointed from the air the previous afternoon, the young officer in charge praying they would find the Storch before the moon rose any higher.

Behind him von Friedel's batman, who had been ordered to go along with the volunteer patrol to identify his master, whispered, 'I can smell something burnt over there — at ten o'clock, *Herr Leutnant*.'

The young officer sniffed the air. There was, indeed, a faint smell of burnt metal and oil. 'This way,' he ordered softly.

Every man's nerves tingling anxiously, they crept forward again, eyes narrowed, trying to pierce the gloom, bodies tensed in anticipation of the first hard thwack of a steel-tipped slug.

'There!' the batman hissed.

'Yes, it's the plane all right,' the lieutenant agreed, 'or what's left of it. You, you … and you, come with me. The rest of you form a perimeter defence.'

Swiftly, the little group began to examine the burnt-out plane, fumbling in the dark, while around them the rest of the patrol went to ground, ready to do battle if necessary.

'The pilot,' one of the infantryman said. 'Over here, *Herr Leutnant*.'

Hurriedly, the officer knelt down beside the corpse, which in spite of the freezing cold, had become bloated with gas. Reluctantly the officer turned over the stinking body, trying not to hear the sighs that came as the gas escaped from the dead man's mouth. For an instant, he clicked on the little torch strapped to his tunic. The swollen, green face looked up at him with unseeing eyes. The tunic bore the flying eagles of the Luftwaffe. 'Yes,' he confirmed the identification, 'it's the pilot all right.' He switched off the torch. 'But where in heaven's name is von Reichel?'

Meanwhile, the soldier checking the wrecked interior of the plane reported, 'Nothing left, *Herr Leutnant*. Just a bit of burnt paper. Looks as if it might have been a flight map.'

'*Gut*. Stick it in your pocket, Heinz. The rest of you spread out now. Von Reichel's body must be here somewhere, unless they captured him.'

Wishing this macabre business was over, the young officer, together with the shaking batman, who had spent his three years of war in higher headquarters, began to search the snow-heavy bushes in a circle around the wreck.

Five minutes later they found what they sought: a rough mound of fresh earth, laboriously carved out of the frozen soil. Swiftly, the infantrymen unbuckled their entrenching tools and started to dig, knowing that every minute they spent in no-man's land increased the risk of their being discovered.

It didn't take long to find the corpse. Obviously the Russians or whoever had buried the missing man had been in a hurry too, for von Reichel was covered by only a few centimetres of soil.

Trying to ignore his own revulsion and knowing that he had to do it if he didn't want to lose face with his hard-bitten stubble-hoppers, the young officer cleared the rest of the earth away from von Reichel's face and then flicked on the blue light. 'Is it your officer?' he demanded.

The batman, obviously terrified out of his wits, gulped, 'I think so … but he looks different than when I…'

'Yes, soldiers usually do when they're dead,' the lieutenant said cynically, his revulsion overcome by contempt for this rear-echelon stallion who had never heard a shot fired in battle. 'Well, is it him, or isn't it?'

'I don't know exactly,' the man quavered. 'But he had a big mole on his right hand … at the back.'

'Holy shit!' the officer moaned, but he remembered General Stumme's precise order to him before the patrol had set out. With a sigh, he fumbled in the cold earth for the corpse's right hand, freeing it with difficulty. 'Is this it?' he asked, holding up the dead man's hand.

'Yes, yes,' the batman answered hastily. 'That's the mole, *Herr Leutnant.*'

'You sure?'

'On my oath, sir.'

The lieutenant flicked off the light. To their right an owl hooted softly three times. It was the agreed-upon signal. Trouble was brewing. 'Come on,' he hissed urgently. '*Los!* Let's make steam. The Ivans are out there…'

'Certainly looks very odd to me, *Herr General,*' Colonel Franz, Stumme's chief-of-staff, said thoughtfully.

The middle-aged general said nothing. Instead he dipped the end of his cigar in looted Crimean brandy and sucked on it reflectively. Outside, telephones rang and typewriters clattered as the staff prepared plans for a new attempt to crush the last Soviet resistance in Stalingrad.

'The pilot shot through the back of the head but unburied, and the plane burnt. But von Reichel buried. Very strange,' Colonel Franz continued. 'I mean, since when have the Ivans shown such respect for our dead as to bury them, especially in no-man's land. And alongside the aircraft, too. General, I think they got von Reichel's map, and this is a fake to convince us they haven't.'

Stumme nodded a little sadly. 'I tend to agree with you. They've got it and that means they know our complete dispositions.' He sighed. 'I am afraid we'll have to inform the Führer HQ.'

Colonel Franz looked at him gloomily. 'Heads will roll, general. You know that the Führer has ordered strictly that no officer carrying top-secret maps should go anywhere near the front?'

'I know it well, my dear Franz.' General Stumme gave him a parody of a smile. 'The head which will roll will be mine.' He picked up the phone. 'Operator, connect me with the Führer HQ — *at once*,' he barked.

General der Panzerwaffe Stumme had just signed his death-warrant.

Hitler patted Blondi, his Alsatian bitch, fondly on the back. 'Sometimes, Linge,' he said to his tall SS valet who accepted the lead dutifully now the exercise period was over, 'I agree with the Great Frederick — the more I see of people, the better I like dogs.'

'Yes, *mein Führer*,' Linge said solemnly.

Hitler patted Blondi on the back once more and then turned and walked back to his headquarters through the tall pines which sheltered 'Werewolf', as the Ukrainian HQ was called, from prying Soviet eyes.

The staff was waiting for him in the simply furnished log blockhouse which was the operations' room, and an irritated Hitler could see immediately that they had made no progress in the 'von Reichel affair', as it was now being called at the HQ.

He stalked by the high-ranking officers with their purple-striped breeches and bemedalled chests and sat down at the head of the table. Without ceremony, he snapped, 'They've got his maps, haven't they, eh?' Wooden-faced Field-Marshal Keitel, whose heavy chin looked as if it might have been cast in a foundry, said unhappily. 'I think so, *mein Führer*.'

Hitler's face contorted in a sneer. 'You *think* so, my dear Keitel.' He poked a thumb at his own chest. 'I *know* so! Have not the Reds a standing order that any captured German officer with the purple stripe of the General Staff down his trousers is to be treated like a king? They know, the NKVD, how to get information out of our people when they've captured them. Believe you me, those Red sadists could make even a mummy talk!'

One of the younger officers ventured a smile and Hitler froze him with a threatening look. On this particular November afternoon, the Führer was in no mood for joking. 'Our men in the Gestapo could learn a thing or two from the NKVD.' Hitler sighed. 'All right, I have already instigated court-martial proceedings against General Stumme. As corps commander he takes the final responsibility for the failings of his officers. Agreed?' He looked around the circle of well-fed faces.

Not one of them dared contradict him although they knew that this meant the end for a gallant officer who had fought bravely for Germany since 1939.

Hitler gave a cynical little smile, and told himself that he had tamed them, these fine officers, with their aristocratic ways and fancy manners. He had them in the palm of his hand. 'Good, then we can assume the worst. They know our exact dispositions. So what will the Reds do?' He answered his own question. 'I shall tell you, *meine Herren*. They will first select our weak spots. What are they?'

Again he answered his own question. 'Our Allies, the weakest link in the chain, those wretched Romanians and Mussolini's shocking spaghetti-eaters.'

There was a mumble of agreement from the staff and cunning-faced Colonel-General Jodl, Hitler's chief-of-operations, said, 'With permission, *mein Führer*, I would suggest the left flank.'

'Exactly, the Romanian Third Army — the weakest spot in the whole front, gentlemen.' Hitler tugged the end of his nose thoughtfully. 'Now the Reds know our exact dispositions down to the level of division, we can expect them to do the following in order to relieve the pressure on Stalingrad. They will resort to their usual tactic of infiltration, probing for the best spot for a major attack. When they have found it, they will reinforce and build up rapidly and hit us hard with massed armour. Now we can't rely on the Romanians to be able to recognize what the Reds are up to — their divisional staff officers are hopeless. No, gentlemen, we must have German troops up there in the north.'

'The barrel is empty,' Keitel replied hastily, preparing Hitler for the surprise Jodl was soon to spring on him. 'Our reserves are exhausted. Paulus's Sixth has eaten them all up completely.'

'Nonsense!' Hitler said sternly and Keitel's face flushed. He lowered his big, wooden head like a naughty child criticized by a village schoolmaster. 'Of course there are reserves. Order a comb-out of the army's rear echelon staff, taking only five per cent of the men employed — *supposedly* — there,' he sneered, 'and I wager you could form a new whole army. But no matter. I don't demand a large force. Just a highly mobile, experienced, motorized combat group, led by a resolute officer with extensive experience on the Eastern Front.' He leaned forward, giving them the full benefit of his confident, hypnotic eyes. 'I want the Führer's Fire Brigade dispatched to the Romanians this very day. They'll do the job if anyone can. And I want them provided with the highest authority so that they can act completely independent of both Paulus and Dumitrescu. The Führer's Fire Brigade has not let me down yet, gentlemen,' he added with a smile at their surprised looks — they hadn't realized that he knew the nickname given to Harsch's elite hunting commando. 'And I doubt if it ever will.'

He started to rise to his feet, but Jodl interrupted him with a polite little cough, '*Mein Führer*,' he said carefully, as Hitler sat down again, 'we of the staff have been considering von Paulus's position in Stalingrad for three days now. In the light of a probable attack on our left flank, which if it only partially succeeded would cut Paulus off from his supplies so that the Luftwaffe would have to feed his men from the air, a very unlikely proposition —'

'*Um Himmelswillen!*' Hitler angrily interrupted the white-faced general. 'Don't be so damned long-winded! What do you want to say?'

'*Mein Führer*, why not withdraw from the Volga and abandon Stalingrad before it is too late?' Jodl blurted out his suggestion.

Hitler stared hard at the general while all round there was a shocked silence as the staff waited for the explosion which was sure to come.

But when Hitler spoke at last, his voice was soft and reasonable, yet there was no mistaking the determination and authority behind his words. 'Colonel-General Jodl, I would sooner take that pistol you bear at your side and blow a bullet through my brains than abandon Stalingrad.'

Jodl opened his mouth as if to speak, but Hitler waved him to be silent.

'There will be no arguments, Jodl. My mind is made up. There will be no withdrawal from Stalingrad as long as I am alive. Ensure that the Führer's Fire Brigade is given its marching orders immediately.' He rose to his feet. 'Gentlemen, I wish you a good afternoon.' Hitler strode out as his staff stiffened to attention.

For what seemed a long time they remained standing thus, like actors at the end of the first act of some nineteenth-century melodrama, until finally Jodl relaxed and said in a quiet little voice, as if he was talking about the state of the weather; '*Kameraden*, if the Ivans get through, it will mean the end of Stalingrad and four hundred thousand soldiers.' He hesitated a fraction of a second, 'It could well mean the end of Germany, too...'

CHAPTER 5

The going was murderous. Doubled up against the wind that howled across the steppe at a hundred kilometres an hour the gulag rats toiled up the steep slope, each man blanketed in an icy cocoon of swirling, vicious white snowflakes.

They had been marching for three hours now, straight into the heart of the great snowstorm, the flakes penetrating every gap in their uniforms, making clumsy icy clumps of their boots, blinding them, whipping their crimson, streaming faces cruelly with razor-sharp particles. But still Katukov, marching at the head of the long strung-out column, would not allow his weary officers to halt the battalion.

'We must be well away from the Don by the time the Romanians discover what happened at the river', he snarled angrily when Boldin had requested a stop.

'But comrade colonel,' Boldin had shouted his protest, 'I doubt if the Romanians will venture out in this kind of weather, and if we go on much longer like this the men will begin falling out!'

'Then we will see what happens when that eventuality arrives,' had been Katukov's reply.

Now that eventuality had arrived. A senior sergeant from the rear company came staggering up out of the white, whirling fog, wheezing for breath like an ancient asthmatic, to report that five men had already fallen out and were refusing to move.

Katukov's expression did not change. 'Vulf,' he commanded, 'keep the companies moving. Boldin, you come with me.'

Together the two officers, their bodies bent against the wind, worked their way along that long line of human misery, the men not even turning to look at the passing officers, each one too preoccupied with his own wretchedness.

Captain Simonvitch, the commander of D Company, was waiting for them in the snow. At his feet were a handful of men some on their knees as if they were praying, others slumped full length in the snow, eyes closed, so that a casual observer might have thought they were asleep — or dead.

'I've tried everything to get them on their feet, comrade colonel,' he said anxiously, his eyes liquid with pain behind the pince-nez he wore. He had been a secondary-school teacher before one of his pupils had denounced him to the NKVD and he had been sent to the camps. 'Threats, pleas, promises,' he wrung his begloved hands like a mother over a naughty child.

Katukov ignored him. Standing there with the wind whipping his greatcoat against his tall, skinny frame, hovering above the fallen men, he cried, 'You are not to fall out, you scum, till I tell you to do so!' He aimed a kick at the nearest rat.

Boldin saw Simonvitch wince as the boot thudded into the fallen man's ribs. The ex-teacher felt for his rats. Indeed he treated his mixed collection of crooks and political prisoners like the kids he had once taught in happier days.

Pitifully, the wretch slumped in the snow raised his head, eyes blank of all emotion, even fear, and croaked, 'Can't go … on … finished … can't go on…' He was too exhausted to complete the sentence. His head dropped once more.

Katukov raised his voice so that they could all hear. 'Listen, you parasites, I am not going to risk the success of this mission for rats like you. I know you — you'd sell your own mothers for a glass of vodka. None of you are going to spill your guts to the enemy if they find you.' He dropped his hand to his pistol-holster.

Simonvitch looked up at him in sudden alarm. 'What are you going to do, colonel?' he asked.

Katukov did not even look at the anxious captain. 'I'm going to give you up to three, and then anyone who is still not on his feet I'm going to shoot.'

'Colonel!' Boldin protested. 'These men are exhausted. You can't do this to them!'

'I can do exactly what I want, Major Boldin. My word is law. I have power of life and death over the scum which I have the misfortune to command.' Expertly he flicked off the holster catch and drew his pistol. '*One!*' he said loudly.

None of the wretches sprawled at his feet stirred.

'*Two!*'

Still there was no movement.

'*Three!*'

Katukov hesitated only an instant. Without appearing to aim, he jerked back the trigger. At his feet the man who had been kicked screamed with agony as the bullet, fired at such short range, blasted a huge hole in his back. His hands grabbed two handfuls of snow and he squeezed them hard in his death throes. His head lolled to one side and he was dead.

'In the name of God, you murdered him!' Simonvitch screeched. 'Murdered him in cold blood!'

'*Ruki nazad!*' Katukov commanded, using the old order from the gulag.

Shocked, Simonvitch placed his hands behind his back, as if he were a prisoner again, waiting the next order of the Greenhat in charge of him.

Katukov stepped over the dead man. 'All right, you have seen I am not making idle threats,' he said, his voice harsh and biting. 'Now, who is next? I warn you, I'd rather shoot every last one of you pigs than leave you here.'

The threat worked. Swaying like drunken men, their faces gleaming with white crystals that hung in thick profusion from eyebrows and moustaches, the exhausted men staggered to their feet and stumbled after the battalion.

Katukov watched them go for a minute, then turned to Boldin, putting his pistol back in its holster as he did so. 'Well?'

'Nothing,' Boldin said. His face revealed nothing of his feelings. With his foot, he started to push snow over the dead body. It would keep the wolves off for a while.

They came across the abandoned farm crouched in a group of firs sparkling a bright white in the gleaming new snow an hour after the snowstorm had stopped. By now even Colonel Katukov had had enough. After an officers' patrol — the officers being the only ones with any strength left — had ascertained that the tumbledown, straw-roofed farmhouse and barn were empty, he gave the command for the gulag rats to settle there for the night.

Now the fires were blazing everywhere, with the gulag rats warming their millet porridge over the flames, standing in weary lines to hold their canteens for a few minutes at the fires. Others were already slumped in the dirty straw, rolling cigarettes and drinking cold tea from their water-bottles, chatting softly with one another.

Boldin and Vulf, sipping in silence the last of the little intellectual's vodka mixed with cold tea, watched the ghost-like queues as they filed past, each face lit for a moment in the glow of the fires. It was a strange pageant of tough, rough, bearded faces: the faces of saints and sinners, Boldin couldn't help thinking, but gulag rats all, whatever their past crimes, condemned to sacrifice their lives out here in this white waste — for what? For Stalin, the man who had sent them to the camps, or for Mother Russia, the country which had created them? Boldin's brow creased in a worried, thoughtful frown. The same old questions had plagued him ever since he had allowed Katukov to recruit him from the gulag. He had still not found an answer after all these months in the line.

Glinka, the red-cheeked battalion comedian who affected an old-style drooping Cossack moustache which he called his 'tea-strainer', was going on about food in his usual cheerful manner. 'For *me*, comrades, food does not need to be of top quality like the Red Army throws away as waste. No, I'm so hungry most of the time, I could eat your smelly boots, Sasha, and wash them down with snow water!'

But this evening not even Corporal Glinka could raise much of a laugh. The march through the snowstorm had been too exhausting and the future out here behind the enemy lines too uncertain. The mood of the men lying in the straw was depressed. Indeed a couple of them were singing softly that melancholy soldiers' song 'The Dugout' with its sad, sentimental words of nostalgia and foreboding:

The flame flickers in the narrow stove.
On the log the resin glitters like a tear
And the accordion in my dugout
Sings to me of your eyes and your smile.
You are now far away, far away,
Between us there are hundreds of kilometres of snow.
You are so far, I cannot come to you
But death is outside, four paces away.
Sing, accordion, sing, defying the blizzard.
Call, call again for the happiness that has gone astray.
It is warm in this cold, cold dugout
It is warm with my undying love.

Boldin drained the last of his tea and vodka and told himself that there was something else, too. In spite of their exhaustion and depression, the rats were angry at the events of the afternoon. If Colonel Katukov pushed them much further, he could well have an open rebellion on his hands, and out here deep behind the Romanian lines all the Greenhats in the world would not protect him from the gulag rats' wrath. He sniffed and dismissed the gloomy thought.

'Wipe the dewdrop off yer hooter, Sasha, or award yourself the Order of the Red Snot! By God, if you could see yerself in a mirror, comrade, you'd never comb yer hair with the light on ever agen!' Glinka laughed uproariously at his own joke.

Boldin buckled his water-bottle on to his belt, 'Vulf, give them thirty minutes more and then order the fires doused. They can be seen kilometres away.'

'*Horoscho*,' Vulf answered dutifully.

Five minutes later Boldin had settled down in the dirty straw next to Katukov, who sat there with his boots off to reveal that his foot-bandages were pink with blood — obviously the march had been too much even for his iron constitution — making a last study of his map by the fading light.

'Tomorrow?' Boldin asked.

Katukov raised his head and grunted, 'The same as today, I should expect, though now we are coming out of the hills, we can anticipate collective farms, inhabited by our own people. If they are patriots and not working with the fascists, I shouldn't be surprised if they couldn't give us the information we need about the presence of the Fritzes in this sector.'

'*If*,' Boldin said a little cynically. As cruel as the Fritzes had been, they had given the peasants back their land, taken off them by Stalin in the early thirties. Most of them, as a result, worked with Fritzes. 'How much further to the bridge at Kalach, colonel?' he added a moment later.

'Forty kilometres or thereabout. Two days' march in these conditions, Boldin.'

The big major looked up at the icy glitter of sky through a hole in the roof. It looked as if the storm had passed. The sky was cold, but clear. 'Yes, you could be right, colonel. With no more snow, we might do it.'

Katukov drew his greatcoat about him. 'We *will* do it, comrade major,' he said coldly. 'Has not Comrade Stalin himself said recently that today an officer's order is an iron law. They obey … or they die! Good night.'

Katukov turned over and dragged his greatcoat over his ears. A minute later he was deep in an exhausted sleep. But Boldin could not go off so easily, in spite of his exhaustion. Whatever the solution to his question — did he serve Stalin or Russia? — might turn out to be, he knew his primary duty at this moment was to his men. Only he could prevent Katukov sacrificing their lives unnecessarily. From now on, he told himself, thinking of the NKVD colonel's last words — 'they obey, or they die' — he must be alert. As long as he lived, there would be no more shootings of helpless men lying in the snow.

At last sleep overcame Boldin. He, too, started to drift, barely hearing the soft crunch of the sentries' felt boots in the snow and a long, long way off a strange hissing sound, which he told himself must be in the wind…

CHAPTER 6

'Major!' the voice hissed urgently.

Boldin woke with a start. He stared wide-eyed into the gloom.

Corporal Glinka's face came into focus, the frost particles glittering in his eyebrows and moustache. 'What's going on?' Boldin said thickly and wiped a sabre-scarred hand across his scummed lips.

'There's somebody out there.'

'What!' Boldin sat up, suddenly very awake. 'Fritzes?'

'*Ya ne znayu*,' Glinka shook his head. 'I don't know. All I know is that they're not our people.'

Hastily, Boldin pulled his boots from beneath his head and thanked God that they hadn't frozen up this time. 'Tell me, what gives?' he whispered urgently, pulling them on.

'Well, comrade,' Glinka said a little hesitantly, 'you know Glinka's guts — they're always empty.'

'Get on with it!'

'I was on sentry patrol, comrade, when my hooter started to twitch, my belly began to growl, and the old jaw-water flooded my chops. Someone out there somewhere was cooking real meat, *real meat!*' He emphasized the words again, as if they were of vital importance. 'So old Glinka —'

'I'll tell you what old Glinka did,' Boldin interrupted him, hastily slipping into his greatcoat and buckling on his pistol holster. 'He left his post, an offence punishable by death on front-line service, and set off to look for the source of that cooking, eh?'

Glinka looked up at him, his head cocked to one side in the comical manner he had and said, 'My family was always known as "the locusts" back home before we got sent to the camps. There was nothing to stop us when we scented vittels.'

In spite of his tension, Boldin grinned. 'All right, locust, what did you discover?'

'There's a camp out there. Ski troops to judge by the skis parked everywhere, all set up in nice little tents like a lot of shitting Young Pioneers, cooking their *real* meat as if it grew on trees, with not a care in the world. There was even one of the greedy swine singing as he filled his mean guts.'

'What language?'

'None that I could identify, comrade,' Glinka said, suddenly gloomy. 'All that *real* meat. By the Holy Virgin, it's enough to sicken a fellow of humanity! It really is!'

Boldin laughed softly and pulled on his fur cap. 'Come on, locust, we'll go and have a look at these *real* meat-eaters of yours.'

Silhouetted against the silver light of the stars and the dying flames of their cooking fires, Major Boldin could just make out the soldiers who were now beginning to creep into their four-men tents, while a handful of others, sub-machine-guns slung over their chests, were spreading out around the camp at an officer's order.

Occasional snatches of conversation drifted across the snowy steppe, but all that the men crouching there in the firs could make of it was that the language wasn't Russian. With frozen fingers Boldin adjusted his night glasses in an attempt to make out the strangers' uniforms. But in that light he could not distinguish them until he spotted the tall plume rising from the hat of the officer issuing the orders to the sentries. 'Of course,' he said, 'the Alpini.'

Next to him Glinka whispered, 'What lot are they, comrade? I thought the English were on our side?'

Boldin laughed. 'No, they're not English, they're Italians.'

'Oh, Musso's boys,' Glinka said, a little relieved. 'They tell me that lot takes their boots off so that they can run faster.'

Boldin shook his head, the smile gone from his face. 'Not those Italians, Glinka. They're Mussolini's elite, the mountain troops. They won't run so easily, believe you me.' He made a hasty count of the number of tents, assessing that each one could hold four men. As there were over a hundred of them, he estimated swiftly that the Alpini were in half-battalion strength. He had seen enough, 'Come on, Glinka, come on. We'd better get back and inform the colonel.'

Glinka pulled a face. 'That's why I woke you, comrade major. You know that Greenhat. He'll be after them like a skinny dog after a fat bone.'

'Perhaps, but there's no other way. As soon as it's light, they'll spot us anyway, and we wouldn't have much of a chance if they come after us on skis.'

Glinka nodded. 'Oh, well,' he whispered, as they started to crawl back the way they had come, 'there might be a bit of grub left over for us in the morning over there.'

Boldin shook his head in mock wonder. 'One day,' he said, 'that skinny gut of yours will be the death of you.'

It was nearly dawn. To the east, the dull white of the sky was beginning to give way to the faint pink of the winter sun still hidden beyond the horizon, but already beginning to flush the snow a dramatic blood-red.

For two hours, the gulag rats had been crawling into their positions until now they surrounded the unsuspecting Italian camp. Their anger and foreboding of the previous day was forgotten at the prospect of the loot and other pickings they might find in the enemy tents. Together with Katukov, Boldin and Vulf surveyed the tented camp. Apart from the sentries who were now beginning to gather wood for, the morning fires, the Italians slept on. They must think this is peacetime,' Vulf commented cynically. 'I wouldn't be surprised if they didn't have a damned bugler to sound reveille.'

'As far as they're concerned,' Boldin said, 'they are deep behind their own lines. Why should they take more than normal precautions against partisans, if such creatures exist in this part of Occupied Russia?' he added for Katukov's benefit.

The grey-eyed colonel frowned at him, but made no comment. Obviously he knew, too, that most of the local peasants supported the enemy; there were no partisans in this part of the Don Basin. 'Remember, no one is to escape to report our presence behind the Romanian lines. Clear?'

'Clear,' the other two answered dutifully.

'The main thing is to keep them away from those skis of theirs. Once they get them on, we've lost them.'

'Don't worry, comrade colonel,' Boldin reassured him, 'we'll see they keep away from the boards.' He rose to his feet. Behind him was his group of Volga Germans, all of whom spoke the German dialect of their peasant forefathers who had come to Russia at the invitation of Catherine the Great in the eighteenth century. 'Shoulder your weapons,' he ordered. The men did as he commanded.

Vulf looked at Boldin as if to say, shall I come with you, little brother?

Boldin shook his head and glanced at Katukov who was now engrossed in the scene to his front. Vulf nodded his understanding. Boldin's look read: 'Keep your eye on the Greenhat; ensure that he doesn't sacrifice the rats unnecessarily.'

Slowly the little group of rats in their German uniforms began to plod across the snow straight towards the tents, while behind the snow-dunes their comrades waited in tense anticipation, knowing that if anything went wrong with Katukov's plan they were dead men.

It seemed to take the Italian sentries an age to spot them. Indeed, they were only fifty metres from the first tent before a sharp voice cried, '*Alto*!'

Boldin halted. Behind him, his men did the same. A dark-faced man with a great beak of a nose was staring at them hard, submachine-gun levelled in the direction of Boldin's grey-clad chest.

Boldin tried to forget that one wrong move and the little Italian could rip him apart at that range. He drew himself to his full height and called as haughtily as he could, '*Italianer, sprechen sie deutsch?*'

'*Como?*' the sentry asked, obviously uneasy in the presence of what looked like a German officer. '*Que dice?*'

'*Offizier … bringen sie mich zum Offizier,*' Boldin barked in his best German officer manner. '*Warum stehen sie noch da?*'

'*Si, si, prego.*' The sentry dropped his weapon a little and indicated they they should advance closer.

'Get ready to run,' Boldin commanded out of the side of his mouth, 'and then hit the dirt — *quick*!'

Striding forward as if he were Hitler himself, Boldin advanced closer to the camp, noting that more and more Italians were emerging into the new day, shivering and slapping their arms about their bodies, their breath a thick grey on the icy air. Now the piles of skis were only a matter of twenty or thirty metres away. They were going to pull it off.

It was just then that an officer came out of a tent to Boldin's right. He paused there, more wide awake than his men, the look of suspicion on his face obvious even at that distance. He opened his mouth to order something. Boldin knew they had been discovered. He didn't wait for the Italian to sound the alarm. Instead he bellowed, '*At the double, comrades!*'

His men needed no urging. They knew what was at stake. They pelted forwards towards the piled skis as the first wild shots erupted and the Alpini were flinging themselves down for cover in the snow.

Now all around the camp the rats rose from their hiding places. Their bayonets flashed in the first slanting rays of the new sun. '*Urrah!*' they cried bravely, and started advancing through the knee-deep snow in the very same instant that Boldin and his Germans flung themselves down around the skis and, panting crazily, began to answer the Italian fire as best they could, slugs striking up flurries of snow all around them.

Teniente Goldwasser knew instinctively that the companies had run into bad trouble. He had just been strapping on his ski boots in the tent that none of his brother officers would share with him because they maintained he was a Jew — which he was, though for his own safety he always stated that he was from the South Tyrol where half the population had German names and were German speaking — when the confused firing had broken out, punctuated by hoarse cries and commands in a language that could only be Russian. He didn't hesitate. Loosening the pistol in his holster, he dragged his skis from beneath his bedroll — like any other Jew living in a fascist country in the year of 1942 he was prepared for any emergency — and started strapping them on, while the cries in Russian grew louder and louder. Then he was ready. With his knife he slashed open the back of the tent. He gasped at the sight of the Russian infantry stumbling clumsily through the deep snow, men falling here and there all along their line, but still coming on all the same, as if nothing could stop them.

Teniente Goldwasser was no hero. He had joined the Alpini because he was an expert skier and liked to ski, and because the uniform was very attractive to the prettier daughters of well-off middle-class families in the capital. Looking round the centre of the camp, he saw immediately that his comrades were trapped. There were already Russians surrounding the skis. Bodies lay writhing and moaning in the snow everywhere.

Now it was every man for himself. *Sauve qui peut.*

Goldwasser seized his poles. There was a slight downward slope behind his tent. It would give him the opportunity to gain speed almost at once. He took a deep breath, counted to three, and then with a grunt thrust himself forward. There was no going back now.

The advancing Russians saw him almost at once, the lone figure hissing across the white surface of the snow, escaping the confused fighting of the camp. 'Stop him!' the cries went up on all sides.

Half a dozen Russians kneeling in the snow began to pump fire at the man whizzing at them. Desperately, Goldwasser zigzagged from side to side, exerting all his skill, his body crouched low as he swept ever nearer, the bullets tugging and plucking frighteningly at his uniform.

Angrily Colonel Katukov took aim, feet spread apart, hand clasped on his hip, as if he were on some peacetime firing-range. The pistol jerked in his hand. Goldwasser yelped with pain and staggered alarmingly.

There was a ragged cheer from the gulag rats. 'You've got him, comrade!' Simonvitch yelled.

The men kneeling in the snow ceased firing. The Italian was obviously finished.

Goldwasser knew he wouldn't get a second chance. He straightened up immediately and thrust forward with all his strength, forgetting the burning pain in his arm where the Russian bullet had struck him. A bearded, angry face under a fur cap loomed up directly in front of him. Hardly aware of what he was doing, Goldwasser struck out with his ski pole.

The gulag rat screamed shrilly and went reeling back into the snow, the cruelly spiked pole sticking out of his eye, and then Goldwasser was through, careening crazily down the long slope ahead with his one remaining pole, the bullets striking up the snow behind him to no purpose.

They were slaughtering the survivors now. In silence Boldin and Katukov watched as the rats, most of them a little drunk on the looted Chianti, streamed after a half-naked Alpini, yelling drunken obscenities, as the little Italian cut in and out of the tents. And then they trapped him…

'Animals,' Simonvitch said thickly and turned away in disgust, tears gleaming behind his pince-nez. 'Revolting animals! What gets into men like that?'

Vulf shrugged cynically. 'Booze,' he said. 'What else do you expect, my tender-hearted friend? They are the gulag rats after all, aren't they?'

Boldin ignored Vulf's comment, just as he ignored the burly gulag rat with the tattooed face of the professional criminal who, with one booted foot planted on a dead Italian officer's chest, was expertly extracting his gold teeth, one after the other, chuckling with delight at his good fortune. The men were brutalized beyond words. Could one expect them to be any different after the years in the camps and these last two years at the front? They had been conditioned to kill in the most bestial way, and all of them knew in their heart of hearts that that was how they would end themselves sooner or later.

With disgust and disdain written all over his face, Boldin turned to Katukov and asked: 'What now?' Katukov took his grey gaze off a gulag rat attempting to saw a dead Italian's finger off with his bayonet in order to obtain the golden wedding ring it bore. 'What do you mean — what now?' he demanded.

Boldin shrugged carelessly, as if the matter really didn't matter very much to him, but still it had to be faced up to. 'One of the Italians got away. Undoubtedly he will report to some authority sooner or later.'

'Report what?'

'That his force was attacked by troops wearing German uniforms. Even the stupid Romanians will be able to work out what such a disguised force is doing so far behind their lines. Result: they'll come looking for us in force.' He nodded at the harsh, blue winter sky with not a snow-cloud in sight. 'Perfect flying weather. They'll have their spotter planes up within hours of that Italian's contacting his own people.'

Katukov bit his bottom lip as if he had just realized the full impact of Boldin's words.

'There is still time, comrade colonel.'

'Time?' Katukov echoed.

'Yes, to turn back. We don't stand a chance in hell if the planes find us out here. It'll be a massacre.'

'Impossible!' Katukov snorted. 'We haven't finished our mission yet. We do not turn back until we reach that bridge and complete our reconnaissance of the terrain.'

'Dead men don't do much marching.'

'Nonsense,' Katukov said, 'we'll find cover by day and march at night. Soon we should come across our own civilians — they will provide the hiding places we will need.'

Boldin shrugged. 'As you command, comrade colonel.'

Five minutes later they set off again, an insignificant black worm of men trailing across that infinite, sparkling white plain with a drunken Glinka singing happily, '*Oh, dear comrades, oh, how I'm gonna enjoy being dead...*'

CHAPTER 7

'The place is inhabited, all right,' Katukov concluded.

'Yes,' Vulf agreed while Boldin continued to study the collective farm in silence. 'You'd think it was peacetime down there, comrade colonel.'

Boldin was tempted to agree. Smoke curled lazily from the little brick houses that surrounded the long low farm of the kind built in the early thirties when Stalin had ordered the collectivization of Soviet agriculture, killing millions of *kulaks* in the process. Boldin could hear the soft lowing of the cows within the barns and a cock crowed triumphantly somewhere. It was indeed all very peaceful, as if the greatest war in history were a million kilometres away and not a mere hundred.

'All right,' Katukov commanded, 'we move in and spend the day there. We march again tonight.'

The company commanders doubled-off back to their companies to carry out the big colonel's orders and Katukov turned to Boldin and Vulf. 'We go in alone. We speak German just in case...' He didn't finish the sentence, but the other two knew well what he meant. A place like that couldn't thrive so peacefully unless it was under German protection.

Ten minutes later their guess was confirmed when dogs and excited children started to stream up the road to meet the column. In their midst a tall man bore the traditional gift of bread, flanked by two pretty girls with braided hair and in peasant costume, carrying bowls of milk.

'But they can see we're Fritzes!' Katukov snorted in exasperation, not wishing to believe what he knew was true: the peasants were indeed collaborating with the enemy.

'Perhaps they're really partisans,' Vulf said, tongue in cheek, enjoying Katukov's discomfiture, 'just waiting for the right moment to attack us.'

Katukov flashed him an angry look. 'We'll play their evil game for a while,' he said through gritted teeth. 'But by God before we leave this night, they'll be taught their lesson! I'll root out these traitors once and for all!'

'*Willkommen, Kameraden,*' the big civilian bearing the bread and salt said in heavily accented German, while the two pretty girls gave a little curtsy to an icy-faced Katukov.

While Boldin and Vulf hid their grins, the civilian tore off a chunk of bread, spread some salt over it in the traditional fashion and handed it to Katukov to eat. '*Essen,*' he commanded.

Katukov choked the piece down and accepted a drink of milk from one of the girls who smiled up winningly at him.

Boldin and Vulf accepted their food and drink too, and Boldin said, this time in Russian, 'Thank you, comrade. Your name?'

'You speak good Russian,' the civilian said, accepting the fact without wonder in the peasant fashion. 'My name is Dudinka, comrade. The people have elected me to be their headman, now that our *natshalnik* has run away.' He gave them a good-humoured smile, as if they knew why he had run off. 'But come comrades, we have room enough to shelter you from this cold. Our food is limited, though.'

'Don't worry,' Boldin reassured the peasant with the strong, generous face, 'we have food enough to supply ourselves.'

'That is good,' Dudinka said, obviously relieved. He turned to the children, who were staring at the soldiers wide-eyed and open-mouthed, 'Hurry, you little brats! Be off with you and warn your mothers to get the kettles boiling. Our German comrades will need hot water for their tea!'

Katukov gave a strangled moan at the words 'German comrades', and a grinning Vulf thought the big crimson faced colonel looked as if he might have a heart-attack at any moment. 'You poor bastards,' he told himself as they started to march towards the farm, their approach heralded by the yelling children running towards the houses and the barking dogs which had appeared suddenly everywhere. 'Katukov's going to toast your balls for this, by God he is!'

'That was our *natshalnik*,' Dudinka said, pointing a calloused finger at the man standing in front of a gleaming new tractor in the centre of yellowing photograph. 'He picked up his heels and ran off when you Germans were over a hundred kilometres away, the bastard!' He spat contemptuously on the floor of the former chairman's office.

Boldin sipped his scalding tea and surveyed the photograph. In spite of its poor quality, he could see that the party official who had run the farm for Moscow had never missed a meal in all his life, unlike the ragged peasants with their wicker-work shoes who now thronged the square outside, chatting with the soldiers and serving them hot water for their tea from great steaming cauldrons.

'He had no neck, like all those Party bosses,' the peasant said. 'All he did was read *Pravda*, talk on the telephone,' he indicated the old-fashioned instrument on the desk, 'and drink tea *with sugar*!' He emphasized the words, as if they were the height of decadent luxury.

Boldin smiled. 'What happened when the Fr — when we Germans came?'

'It was not too bad, comrade. They hanged one or two of the little *natshalniks* who were in the Party. A couple of them got drunk and raped widow Zhukova, though I don't suppose she minded much. I wager she hadn't had it these twenty years and more than once she's offered one of the farm lads a few kopecks to come and help her out,' He winked knowingly at Boldin, who grinned back at him. Boldin liked the big peasant with the grizzled hair and weathered face of a man who had worked hard all his life in the outdoors.

'And then?'

They went away and left us to get on with things the best we could. So the others elected me. But I'm no *natshalnik*,' he added hastily. 'I just organize the plant. Now each and every one of us farms for himself like we did in the old days before that monster in the Kremlin entered our poor lives.' Boldin handed him a cigarette and he nodded his thanks. 'I know not what kind of man your Hitler is, but I tell you this, comrade, there is nothing more precious than freedom! Poor we are, but we are free.' He lit the *Kasbek* cigarette with a flourish and breathed out a stream of blue smoke. 'I think it is better to be dead than not free, comrade.'

Boldin turned away hastily so that the big peasant should not see the look on his face at that moment.

'So, so,' Katukov said, as Boldin reported his news, 'the Fritzes came and went and left the treacherous swine in peace. And have there been Fritzes here since?'

'No, apparently not. Occasionally a few Romanians have passed through, demanding food and the like, but when the peasants could show they had little more than eggs and a few scraggy chickens — they'd hidden their cows and horses, needless to say — they passed on and left them in peace.'

Katukov frowned out of the window at his men chatting to the peasant girls or lounging in the square, smoking their cigarettes and eyeing the little *isbas* as if they were calculating how much loot the poverty-stricken thatched houses might possibly contain. 'In peace,' he echoed. 'Yes, that's just what those *kulak* pigs would like, eh? To be left here to feed their miserable faces on the fat of the land, trying to forget what is happening outside, while the Soviet Fatherland bleeds to death and millions of brave soldiers die for them!'

'For *them*?' Vulf snapped, his weak eyes blazing behind the thick hornrims. Boldin flashed him a warning look.

'We Russians are not dying for common *kulaks* like that, comrade colonel,' he said with surprising boldness. All round, the company commanders tensed.

'What do you mean, comrade lieutenant?' Katukov barked.

'I mean, they, we, all of us — we're dying for one thing only! We're dying for Old Leather Face. It is as simple as that, comrade.' He stared defiantly at Katukov. 'I don't think you are an unintelligent man, although you are a Greenhat. You must understand *that*! We are all being sacrificed in the name of greed, power, ambition — the greed, the power, the ambition of that man in the Kremlin!'

Katukov did not react in the manner that the officers expected. He did not explode or roar with fury at the little red-faced intellectual, whose skinny chest heaved violently, as if he had just run a great race. Instead he said, his voice icy but calm, 'Comrade Vulf, I know you were sent to the gulag because of political crimes —'

'Yes,' Vulf sneered, 'I told my students that the sun didn't exactly shine out of Stalin's arse, or words to that effect. If you can call that a political crime!'

Katukov ignored the interruption. 'But I had thought that you had conquered that, overcome what one might call the follies of youth. I see now that I am wrong. You are as opposed to our great Soviet system *now* as you were in that year of 1939 when the judges were wise enough to sentence you to ten years in the camps. You are just as much a traitor as those peasant swine out there. The only difference between you and them is that they are traitors to our beloved Soviet Fatherland with their bellies, you do so with your head — and that is far, far more dangerous.'

'And what are you going to do about it, Katukov?' Vulf said boldly, too carried away with anger to be afraid now.

Katukov remained icily calm. His hand dropped down to his holster. 'What we of the NKVD always do with traitors, Vulf. I can — and will, if necessary — shoot you.' He made the threat with a voice that was completely devoid of emotion.

Vulf laughed suddenly and Boldin felt a cold finger of fear trace its way down his spine at that strange sound in that place. Vulf was deliberately challenging Katukov. This was the moment of truth.

'My dear Katukov,' he said very grandly, 'how many Greenhats are there here in this God-forsaken place?'

'What in three devils' name is that supposed to mean?'

'This! There is only one of you. There are eight hundred of us. The odds are slightly in our favour.'

Katukov looked down at the skinny little Vulf from his great height, and although Boldin hated all that he stood for, he could not help but admire him. The colonel was completely unafraid, in spite of the fact that he had to know that Vulf was right. 'So that's it, is it?' he said coolly. 'You are relying on that scum out there, are you, *Comrade* Vulf? You think they are going to support you.' He swung round on the other officers who stood there, faces frozen, holding their breath expectantly. 'Or any of you others, for that matter, eh?' He laughed scornfully. 'You think there is honour among thieves, Vulf. Well, you're wrong. Badly wrong.' He flashed a glance at his watch. In an hour it would be dark. The former collective farm had outlived its usefulness. He could act now and show these rebellious swine how vain their hopes really were. Without another word, he strode to the window and ripped it open, sending the snow showering everywhere.

'What are you going to do, comrade colonel?' Boldin asked in alarm.

Katukov ignored him. Instead he leaned out and cried: 'Hey, you scum!'

Everywhere heads turned in his direction. Senior NCOs threw away their cigarettes and snapped to attention.

'They have vodka here, hidden, of course, and they have food!' Katukov cried. 'Take it!'

There was a low cheer from the gulag rats and a moan from the civilians present, followed by cries of protest and fear.

'The women, too, they're yours!' Katukov yelled. 'Do with them what you will. But afterwards, destroy everything. Two of you to a house, smash everything! Windows, doors, gates, chairs, pots, *everything*. Leave them nothing. Not even a pot to piss in!'

A cry rose on all sides as the gulag rats broke ranks, streaming into the narrow lanes between the houses and the farm, pulling out their bayonets and entrenching tools as they ran, slashing at picket fences and smashing in doors and windows. Children screamed and ran for cover. Women fell to their knees and prayed for mercy. But there was none to be had.

They found the collective's supply of vodka, great fifty-litre carboys in wickerwork cases. With their rifle butts they smashed off the necks and grunting mightily poured the fiery spirit down their throats, the liquid running down their unshaven chins and staining the front of their blouses.

Drunk now, they began to splash kerosene from the farm's store on to the straw roofs of the *isbas*. When the peasants tried to stop them, a rifle butt smashed into the protestors' faces put an end to their cries.

The first wisp of grey smoke streaked upwards, becoming scarlet angry flame almost instantly, hissing from roof to roof, the straw crackling wildly. The drunken soldiers staggered backwards, their faces seared by the tremendous heat. Above them, black smoke thrashed and writhed, swinging evilly to the horizon.

Mesmerized like the rest, Boldin watched as a lone figure ran screaming towards the soldiers, a hayfork in his hands, zigzagging in between the dying on the ground. It was Dudinka, the man who less than a couple of hours before had told him it would be better to be dead than unfree. '*No!*' Boldin called aloud, feeling the nails of his right hand bite deep into the palm of his other hand. 'No, don't do it, man!'

But it was too late. Dudinka lunged with his hayfork in the way he had been heaving hay on board the hay-cart these last forty years. A gulag rat holding an empty can of kerosene screamed shrilly as the six prongs sank deep into his back. His can fell from nerveless fingers and he sank to his knees, head bent as if he were in prayer. The prongs came out gleaming bright, wet-red in the wild light of the ever-growing flames.

The rats were on Dudinka before he could strike again, smashing their rifle butts into his big body. Vainly the civilian tried to keep on his feet. To no avail. They hammered him to the ground, and he disappeared beneath their flailing feet. Boldin turned away, sickened.

'So you see, *comrades*,' Katukov sneered over the word, 'if you want to kill me, you will have to do it without the aid of that drunken scum out there.' He jerked his head contemptuously at the gulag rats now being kicked into the column once more, their faces sullen and hangdog after the destruction of the village which still burnt softly in the background, the crackle of the flames punctuated by the sobs of the abused women and the moans of the wounded. 'They are out for themselves, each and every one of them. The only thing which keeps them together is fear — fear of me!'

Boldin was overcome by an overwhelming loneliness, the desolation of the winter world and himself. Around him his fellow officers looked numbly at their boots, not able to face that coldly triumphant face.

Katukov raised his voice. 'All right, we go, *comrades*. But remember this, from now onwards in Punishment Battalion 333, it is march or croak... *Forward*!'

BOOK TWO: *THE BRIDGE AT KALACH*

CHAPTER 1

'Champers, Igor!' *Obersturmbannführer* Harsch ordered his Ukrainian batman, who had been watching the removal of the bullet from *Teniente* Goldwasser's arm with fascinated eyes.

'*Mais non, mon colonel,*' Duclos, the Fire Brigade's doctor protested, dropping his surgical scissors on to the table of the little peasant cottage which housed Harsch's HQ. '*Il est blessé.*' He tapped the bandage lightly and immediately it stained pink.

'Perk him up, I shouldn't wonder,' Harsch said lightly and with his one hand swung the broken infantry sword that he had carried with him now for three years of war.

Igor came in, rubbing the snow off the bottle of champagne and began pouring out three mugs of bubbling, pale-yellow liquid.

Harsch accepted his eagerly. 'Champers, best drink in the world, gentlemen.' He raised his mug, 'Up the cups,' he toasted, 'the night's going to be cold! *Prost!*'

'*Prost,*' the other two said a little reluctantly and sipped their champagne, watching the big scar-faced SS officer with the cropped hair drain his as if he were very thirsty.

'So,' Harsch said, picking up his sword again and swinging it to and fro happily, 'your companies were attacked by a group of Russians. You are sure they were regular Russian troops and not those damned, sneaking partisans?'

'*Jawohl Obersturmbannführer,*' Goldwasser said in his thick Tyrolean German. They were in uniform.'

'Good. How many?'

Goldwasser shrugged, winced with pain, and wished he hadn't. 'My guess would be about a battalion. They swamped the Alpini — and there were four hundred of us.'

'I see.' Harsch nodded to a waiting Igor. The squat Ukrainian, who was one of a dozen different nationalities which made up the Führer's Fire Brigade, refilled the mugs.

For a while the three of them drank in silence while outside the storm howled and the drivers of the half-tracks turned over their motors once again to prevent them freezing up in the bitter cold. Harsch told himself that his men would need an extra ration of *schnaps* before the night was out. Then he walked over to the table, on which was spread his map, and stared down at it hard, swinging the broken sword, which was his habit when he was thinking.

Now as he stared down at the map of the Don Basin, covered with a rash of blue and red pencil marks, the pieces of the jigsaw puzzle began to make some sense in his mind. The Ivans who had attacked the Alpini had to be the same ones who had swept through the Romanian positions on the Don; only half an hour before the wounded Goldwasser had staggered into their camp, the Luftwaffe had reported one of the freed farms burning in the middle of the steppe.

He put the blade of his sword on the map and traced an imaginary line along it, from the Don to the spot on the steppe where the farm had been. Yes, they had to be the same Ivans. But where were they heading? He frowned, following the course of his sword-blade until its jagged edge rested on the River Don once more, close to the small town of Kalach. Of course! The link between the Romanian Third Army and von Paulus's Sixth — *the bridge at Kalach*!

'*Meine Herren*,' he said briskly, 'I think we shall call an end to the doctoring for this night.'

Duclos put down his mug. 'We march, *mon colonel?*' asked the former French army doctor, who had volunteered for the SS from a POW camp.

'Yes. I think I know where those Ivans are heading — and I want to be there before them.'

Goldwasser straightened up in his chair. '*Obersturmbannführer*, would you take me with you?' He hesitated, his mind a mixture of fear and hatred at the outrage the Russians had committed on the Alpini. 'I have a score to pay back.'

Harsch opened his mouth to refuse, then he laughed in that cynical manner of his and tucked his empty sleeve into his belt in preparation for the move. 'Why not, Goldwasser, eh? The Führer's Fire Brigade is a home for half the rogues of Europe. Might as well have a Jew in it as well!' Laughing uproariously, the big one-armed SS officer drained the last of his champers and went out into the howling night.

Obersturmbannführer Harsch had lost his arm in the abortive drive on Moscow in December 1941. His company had been ambushed by a whole regiment of Siberian riflemen. For ten hours he had held them off and then, with a handful of survivors, he had broken out of the trap, his shattered arm hanging by a few shreds of flesh. They had begun the long trek through the snowbound countryside trying to find the broken, retreating German army which had attempted to capture the Soviet capital and failed.

On the first day of that terrible trek, five of his men had died of exhaustion and he had sawed off the arm with an infantry bayonet, his teeth biting into a cartridge to prevent him screaming out loud and revealing their position to the Russian scouts who seemed to be everywhere in the whirling white waste.

On the second day, two of his men went mad with the strain and a third wandered off, his end announced by one lone shot; on the third day the remaining two men killed themselves in a suicide pact and he was alone and weaponless save the broken sword that had belonged to his grandfather. For two further days he staggered, and in the end crawled through that desolate Russian wilderness, the cruel white world glimpsed through a red mist of agony, half-conscious most of the time. Finally he was picked up by a paymaster and his staff who had gone back in the wake of the retreating army to loot the war chest left behind by one of the infantry divisions.

Three months he had lain in the Charité Hospital in Berlin while the great Professor Sauerbruch himself had attended to his self-amputated arm and lesser surgeons had removed his frost-bitten toes. 'I mean, what use are the damn little pinkies anyway?' he had said easily when Sauerbruch had revealed to him that the green, suppurating, stinking pieces of flesh would have to go. 'At least, *Herr Professor*, I'll be able to take a size smaller in shoes now.' Then he had been discharged into a military world which apparently no longer needed his services.

For a month he had hobbled around Berlin on his canes, with the Knight's Cross of the Iron Cross at his throat, trying to obtain a new command, being dismissed politely but firmly everywhere as unemployable at the front.

Himmler, the chief of the SS, had even suggested he should request his release from the Black Guards and apply to run one of the stud farms for willing German maidens and the 'blonde beasts' on leave from the front that he was currently setting up in suitably remote areas of the Reich. They were to provide the Führer with 'the master race of the future'…

'Pimping for those plain-faced horrors of Hitler maidens!' he had exploded to his cronies of the surgical ward afterwards,

'*Gott im Himmel*, I'd rather offer my arse to you lot of vaseline merchants than that!'

But that eventuality had not come about. In the summer of 1942 when the casualties on the Russian Front began to run into hundreds of thousands, someone on Himmler's planning staff came to the conclusion that not only Germans were 'Aryans', but also Belgians, Dutchmen, Norwegians, even Frenchmen and Belgians too — Ukrainians as well, if one closed an eye to those high Slavic cheekbones which marked a 'sub-human' and 'third-class citizen'.

By the end of July 1942, *Obersturmbannführer* Harsch found himself in command of a battlegroup of new SS men, recruited from over half of Europe, its ranks filled with eager, bold youths, desperate to die in the great 'European crusade against the Soviet animal'.

And die they did, in half a dozen bold missions behind the Russian lines which made the headlines in the daily newspapers back in the Reich and gained for Harsch and his new command the nickname, 'the Führer's Fire Brigade'.

This, then, was the man that Hitler had sent out, unwittingly, to stop the gulag rats: big, tough, cynical, an officer who knew he would not survive his war, just as his grandfather and his father had not survived their wars before him; but an officer who would sell his life and that of his men dearly...

CHAPTER 2

Obersturmbannführer Harsch was not the only one that night who was interested in the whereabouts of Colonel Katukov and his vaunted gulag rats. Many hundreds of kilometres behind the front, the Soviet dictator, Stalin, faced his greasy-haired chief of secret police, Beria, and asked that overwhelming question — the one that was being asked everywhere that first week of November 1942 in the offices of the *Stavka*: 'Are the Fritzes backing up the Romanian fascists or are they not, Comrade Beria?' He sucked at his curved pipe and looked at his fellow Georgian with those dark, cunning eyes of his. 'What news do you have of this Colonel … Katukov of yours?' Beria dabbed his brow with his cologne-soaked handkerchief, as scared of the dictator as were the young virgins Stalin was in the habit of dragging from the streets of Moscow — 'the green fruit', he called them. 'Little, comrade secretary,' Beria confessed in an anxious voice.

'How little, my dear comrade?' Stalin asked, his voice silk-soft, his eyes twinkling in that avuncular manner depicted in the standard portrait of him that adorned every Party office wall and 'House of Culture' throughout the Soviet Union. 'Be so good as to tell me, comrade.'

Beria extended his hands outwards in the Georgian fashion. 'I must confess that since he and his battalion broke through the Romanian fascists' line on the Don, we have heard nothing from him.'

'Do you think he has gone over to the Fritzes?' Stalin asked, bending forward in the throne-like chair that glittered under the great czarist candelabra above his head. 'After all, his command consists of known traitors.'

Beria shook his head with more confidence than he felt. His own word was all-powerful in Russia, but he knew the pock-marked dictator had more power than he would ever possess. The executioners with the heavy pistols could appear the moment Stalin clapped his hands together. 'No, comrade. He is a strange one, not at all your typical NKVD man... But one thing is certain, he has ambition, an appetite for glory.' He smiled suddenly at the memory of the day he had summoned the tall, grey-eyed colonel to his office in 1941 and ordered him to form the gulag rats from the scum of the camps to defend the hard-pressed capital. 'Oh yes, glory means more to him than his very life, that one.'

Stalin, sucking at his pipe, considered the information. Finally he said, 'Time is running out, comrade. We must hurry your Greenhat along. What do you think would do the trick, eh — a bauble for the breast or pepper up the arse?' His eyes narrowed cunningly as he stared at Beria and left him to make the decision: medal or bullet.

Beria screwed up his face and tried desperately to out-think the pock-marked monster facing him. Katukov was loyal, he knew that well enough. That one would never falter in his duty in spite of the fact that his command was composed of criminals and traitors, but cut off behind enemy lines there was no one with the knout to make him move more quickly.

'Time is running out,' Stalin said once again.

Beria made up his mind. 'Comrade, I am sure that we can rely on Katukov one hundred per cent, but just to ensure that he realizes the full urgency of his mission, I shall send him an emissary.'

'An emissary?'

'Yes, from Smersh.'

Stalin beamed. 'Smersh, eh. So it is to be the bullet after all, Beria?'

Beria nodded slowly, knowing that his hand had been forced. 'Yes, comrade, if necessary, it will be the bullet...'

Now north of the Don, the Red Army continued their build-up. At night long trains steamed into the makeshift stations from Moscow and even from the Urals, laden with fresh troops. Heavy artillery by the hundreds, thousands of tanks, tens of thousands of fresh horses for the cavalry were brought in on flat cars on the lines running to Serafimovich and Kletskaya. Tirelessly, the *politruks* worked on the men of the attack armies, infusing them with the necessary fanaticism they would need to lay down their lives for Stalin, as undoubtedly many thousands of them would. Each new reinforcement was paraded before the banners of his regiment to receive his rifle or submachine-gun in a formal ceremony. The brass bands blared, martial songs were sung by the soldiers' choirs, and Party officials read out fiery speeches on the vital need for devotion to the Soviet Fatherland to the ranks of grey-clad soldiers standing to attention in the deep snow, their breaths fogging on the icy air.

As the men and materials moved inexorably towards the new front, German intelligence could not fail to see their spoors. Reconnaissance planes spotted the new concentrations, Russian deserters told interrogators of the arrival of new divisions from the east, deep-range Romanian patrols beyond the Don brought back reports of the ever-increasing build-up. But the commander of the Sixth Army in Stalingrad, von Paulus, seemed unmoved by the news of the Soviet build-up brought him by his intelligence officers. Indeed, as that first week of November 1942 drew to a close with the danger of a catastrophe looming ever larger, he issued a self-satisfied proclamation to his weary troops. It read:

The summer and autumn offensive is successfully terminated after taking Stalingrad... The Sixth Army has played a significant role and held the Russians in check. The winter is now upon us... The Russians will take advantage of it. It is unlikely that the Russians will fight with the same strength as last winter...

Behind his back at the Sixth Army HQ, staff officers told each other the Old Man had to be crazy. The Sixth Army could probably tackle the Russians whatever their strength, but weren't its flanks guarded by third-class troops from the Axis armies? What if the Ivans hit them? That week, the gentlemen with the purple stripe of the staff down their elegant breeches shook their heads in disbelief and commented, 'Friedrich von Paulus seems to be whistling his way past the graveyard...'

And in their freezing trenches, the bearded, emaciated infantry stared bleary-eyed across the shell-pitted snowy waste of no-man's land and waited for the inevitable.

Beneath ten metres of earth and concrete, General Chuikov waited too. Two whores had set up a little light housekeeping to the rear of the bunker in a tiny room, its sole furniture an army mattress on the dirt floor, a hissing kerosene lamp which burnt twenty-four hours a day and an old gramophone on which they played the same record time and time again as their officer customers came and went, came and went.

Chuikov tolerated the whores, though he was wont to say in his tenser moments, 'Those bitches are only waiting for the Fritzes to come and give them the pox, too!'

He waited, listening to the exotic music of a continent he would never see, scratching his eczema, drinking moodily most of the day, and asking himself that same old question over and over again: *Where were the gulag rats?*

CHAPTER 3

'The bridge at Kalach' Colonel Katukov announced proudly, as if the double-span bridge down below represented something of value. But then Boldin supposed it did. The gulag rats had marched through more than a hundred miles of enemy-held territory and had discovered the information that Chuikov wanted so vitally: there were no significant German fighting units on this side of the Don. The positions the Red Army would attack were held entirely by second-rate Romanian troops. In silence, the two men crouching in the windswept firs surveyed the area of the key bridge with their glasses, holding one free hand above them so that they did not sparkle in the bright winter sunshine and give their position away.

To the left and right of the bridge's exit on the far side of the river there were sandbagged positions which housed light flak cannon, obviously for use against attacking dive-bombers. Beyond, there was a small collection of little wooden huts grouped around a large stone building which, to judge from the flag flying stiffly in the breeze above it, was the Fritzes' HQ. On their side of the river there was a single sentry, muffled up in a greatcoat with a scarf tied around his helmet, who, hands in pockets and rifle slung carelessly over his shoulders, stamped his feet and watched some comrades of his on the far side throwing snowballs at each other like overgrown schoolboys.

'Rear echelon,' Boldin commented contemptuously. 'They're having a nice old time of it down there, aren't they?'

Katukov did not answer, his lips moving as if he were counting.

Boldin sniffed and dismissed the Fritzes. 'Well, comrade colonel, we've got a long haul in front of us back to our own lines. I suggest we get started and make the most of the darkness. It'll be dusk in an hour, once that sun goes over the hills.'

Katukov continued to count and Boldin could see that while he did so he was thinking hard. Finally the colonel said, 'I make them out to be about hundred. And we are eight hundred. We outnumber them by eight to one.' He lowered his glasses and looked at Boldin, as if the numbers were of some significance.

'Yes. So?'

'What if we decided to disobey orders, Boldin,' Katukov said slowly.

'Disobey orders?'

'Yes. Why run the risk of being attacked on our way back to our lines and the chance of not being able to pass on the information that the Sixty-second Army needs? Why not do it this way: capture the bridge and pass on the information by their radios — the Fritzes always have radios, even the smallest of their units.'

'Capture the bridge!' Boldin exploded, his eyes incredulous. 'But today's only the tenth of November. The attack doesn't start until the nineteenth. We couldn't hold it that long, colonel! That bridge is of vital strategic importance for them. Once they know that we've got it, they'll fall on us like a ton of bricks.'

'But do they need to know, Boldin?' Katukov said calmly. 'We are wearing German uniform and we have enough German-speakers in our ranks. Once it is in our hands, we would allow things to carry on as always so that there would be no suspicion of what had taken place. After all, it is a small, insignificant garrison at present. Why should there be any kind of superior officer coming to inspect the place who might become suspicious, eh?'

Boldin opened his mouth to protest again and then he stopped, bottom lip drooping a little stupidly. There was something to Katukov's sudden plan. In the two or three days it would take them to reach their own lines, there was a distinct possibility that the enemy air force might spot them — with disastrous results. For all he knew, the Romanians were already searching for them, warned by the fleeing Italians or anyone who might have escaped from the burning collective farm.

'I am sure, Boldin,' Katukov appealed to him, 'that we can play-act without suspicion or danger until the curtain for the real spectacle arises on the nineteenth.' He smiled coldly, obviously pleased with his plan and his metaphor.

'There are problems,' Boldin said guardedly.

'Probably, but they can be worked out. Boldin, you know as well as I do that one third of the art of soldiering is simply knowing one's job; another third, the possession of good, sound common sense; the final third is luck. Frederick the Great, the Prussian, once said he had no use for officers who had no luck.' His voice rose. 'Boldin, I have had luck the whole way so far. I know I am going to be lucky again, I can feel it in my very bones.'

'Comrade colonel, that might well be,' Boldin commented coldly. 'But it won't be *your* bones that will suffer if anything went wrong down there, it will be those of my gulag rats.'

'That may well be, but Boldin give me this victory, *please.*'

Boldin could see the naked greed in Katukov's eyes and told himself the Greenhat still craved as much for glory and recognition as he had done the very first day they had met.

'I am no longer young, Boldin. I have devoted my life to the Party cause, and I am still a mere colonel in charge of a bunch of criminals. Time is running out and I must have success if I am to make general before this war is over.' There was no mistaking the note of pleading in Katukov's voice.

'All right,' Boldin said. 'We'll give you your success, but promise me this.'

'Anything!'

'If you do get promotion to the rank of general and are given another command, you will recommend me as your successor in charge of Punishment Battalion 333.'

'Of course, of course, little brother,' Katukov answered eagerly. 'I did not think you had that kind of ambition.'

'I haven't,' Boldin said coldly. 'I am a gulag rat and I will remain one, with one loyalty and ambition only — to look after my men and ensure that their lives are not tossed away worthlessly.' He held out his hand. 'Promise?'

Katukov took it and pressed it hard. 'Promise.'

Unwittingly Colonel Katukov had just signed his own death-warrant.

With dramatic suddenness, the pale yellow ball of the winter sun flashed one more time on the whipping aerials which marked the Fritzes' radio shack and disappeared beyond the hills, plunging the steppe into inky darkness. It was time to go. 'All right,' Boldin whispered, 'boats out!'

The men needed no urging. They had been hiding in the reeds at the edge of the river for two hours now, directly opposite the radio shack which was the attackers' first priority, even before the bridge itself. It had to be secured before the operator could signal what was happening at this lonely little steppe village. Silently, their equipment muffled, their boots covered in rags, they pushed out the rough canoes, abandoned a year before by some unknown fisherman when the Germans had first marched this way and, using their entrenching tools as paddles, started to propel the ugly little craft across.

In the bow of the first, Boldin cocked his head to one side and listened with bated breath for the first sign that the Fritzes had been alerted to their presence. But none came.

From the huts there came shouts and cries, but Boldin knew that it had nothing to do with them. The Germans were having their dinner in spite of the fact that it was only three-thirty in the afternoon.

Five minutes later the bow of the canoe ground to a stop in the snowy, muddy reeds of the other bank. Boldin flung a glance at the stark black silhouette of the bridge some 300 metres to their right. The sentry and the gunners had not moved, and the barrels of the flak cannon still pointed skywards. They had landed undetected. Hastily he cupped his hands around his mouth, now bare of his precious false teeth, which were wrapped in a handkerchief and safely stored in his trousers' pocket, and cawed three times in the fashion of the wild birds of the steppe.

From behind them on the other side of the river came back the answering signal. Now Katukov would move the rest of the battalion to both sides of the bridge. Once his flare signalled they had taken the radio shack, he would double forward, the gulag rats using the stone pillars beneath it to cross and surprise the gunners.

'Follow me!' Boldin hissed. 'Remember they *must* not send a message out to their people.'

Behind him Corporal Glinka grinned evilly and whispered. 'Don't worry, comrade major, they won't.' His long curved knife gleamed a dull silver in the faint light. 'First I'll slit me a Fritz's throat and then I'll cut me a big piece of that salami of theirs. My guts are doing flip-flops at the very thought.' He belched in anticipation.

'Watch some Fritz doesn't cut a piece of your salami off,' Boldin warned. 'Come on!'

In silence they stole forward, ignoring the noise coming from the houses where the Fritzes were feeding, intent solely on the radio shack. Already it was blacked out for the night so that its occupants could not see the killers approaching them over the frozen snow, slinking from shadow to shadow like grey timber wolves. Whatever little noise they made was drowned by the chatter of morse, broken occasionally by a burst of static or metallic voices from far away.

At the edge of the hut, Boldin hissed to Glinka, 'All right, take three men and slip round the other side to check if there's a back door. I'll take the front.'

'*Horoscho*,' the ever-hungry NCO whispered, his face serious and alert now.

On the tips of his toes, Boldin, followed by the rest of the little group, crept round the front of the radio shack, the hand with which he held the long combat knife wet with sweat.

Still nothing moved inside and the chatter of morse continued unabated.

Now the front door was only an arm's length away. In an instant Boldin would reach out for the rough knob, turn it and careen inside, with the old cry on his lips that he had used so many times in house-to-house combat these last terrible months, '*Hände hoch!*'

But that wasn't to be. Just as he reached out to turn the knob, the door opened! A knife of yellow light slid out into the darkness. A big man with his braces dangling, a handful of torn newspaper in his hand, stood there blinking at the sudden inky light, obviously attempting to locate the site of the latrine.

Boldin, frozen in the shadows, heard him draw in his breath and knew instinctively they had been discovered. '*Hey* —'

Boldin dived forward, knife at the ready, bringing the big man down with the force of the impact, the cry of alarm dying on his lips as he fell heavily into the frozen snow.

But in spite of his size, the German signaller reacted more quickly than Boldin anticipated. Just as he raised his knife to strike the lethal stab, the German smashed his doubled fist wildly into the Russian's face. Boldin was dazed for a moment. He had a blurred impression of the German's brutish face shivering before him then he recalled the danger the mission was in if the Fritz succeeded in breaking loose.

With all his strength he brought his body to bear on the German's. The long knife held tightly to his right hip slid into the Fritz's guts. He heaved wildly, his spine taut as if he were racked by the throes of passion. Grimly Boldin held on to him as the man tried frantically to free himself of that terrible blade of steel. Boldin's other hand clamped over the German's mouth to drown the strangled cries coming from his throat. Abruptly the German went limp, his head flopped to one side. He was dead.

Gasping as though he had just run a great race, his whole body trembling, for Boldin could never become accustomed to killing in this manner, he staggered to his feet, swaying wildly as he did so.

Glinka loomed up at the other side of the open door. He eyes fell on the bloody weapon in Boldin's shaking hand, but he made no comment.

Boldin nodded.

Glinka acted straight away. His boot slammed against the door and smashed against the side of the wall. The next instant

Glinka sprang inside. A scream. A yell. A harsh command in Russian and then Boldin was inside with the rest.

A fat, pale-faced German lay moaning on the floor, holding his pudgy white hands to his stomach, through which trickled bright red blood. At the radio, a tall skinny fellow was standing bolt upright, his hands extended to the full limit, as if he were trying to reach the sky, mumbling in a panic-stricken voice, '*Nicht töten Kamerad... nicht töten... Ich bin Kommunist...*' And sitting calmly at the table, Glinka was cutting himself a thick slice off the salami he had surmised would be in the shack with his knife, its blade still dripping red with the blood of the fat German.

Boldin shook his head. 'You could have at least wiped the blade, Glinka,' he commented.

'Adds to the flavour,' Glinka said easily and then turning on the skinny German cried. 'Shut up about communists, Fritz! I eat *them* for breakfast.'

The skinny German shut up like a clam.

The flare hushed into the night sky and burst with startling suddenness, bathing the bridge in its red-glowing eerie light.

It was the signal. Boldin had captured the radio shack successfully. Katukov waited no longer. He rose from the reeds, pistol in hand, and yelled, 'Attack!'

'Attack!' The officers down at both sides of the bridge echoed the excited command. NCOs' whistles shrilled.

'*Urrah!*' the gulag rats roared in a deep, unified bass and started forward.

The sentry on their side of the bridge raised his rifle. But he never had a chance. The tide of rushing, crying men swamped him. He went down, trampled to death by their racing feet. At the gun pits, the terrified crews whirled the handles of their

20mm flak cannon furiously, trying to bring the barrels to bear on the running men who had appeared so frighteningly out of nowhere. To no avail. In a flash the gulag rats were among them, bayonets and entrenching tools flashing, hacking, gouging, chopping. It was over within seconds and the rats raced on, leaving the gun pits filled with dead men.

Katukov ran at the head of the little group, including Vulf, detailed to capture the HQ, knowing that if he weren't there, his prison scum would massacre every German they found.

On all sides now there was confused fighting in the darkness.

The startled Germans opened up from the windows of their huts or attempted to close with the Russians in the tiny streets. Scarlet flame stabbed the blackness. Men screamed and tumbled to the ground. No quarter was given or expected. When Russian and German clashed, they fought to the death, trampling and kicking the men at their feet, crazy animal grunts issuing from their throats.

A stick grenade sailed through the air in front of Katukov. '*Duck!*' he cried urgently. The grenade exploded in a flash of angry purple flame. Shrapnel zinged through the air. The blast hit Katukov across the face like a blow from a flabby fist. Behind him one of the rats howled in agony and dropped to the ground. Katukov raced on.

A German in long, drooping underpants appeared at the door of the HQ. Katukov pressed the trigger of his pistol. The German slammed against the door and started to trail slowly down its length, his false teeth bulging absurdly from his mouth. Katukov sprang inside. A sergeant stood at the far end of the corridor, rifle held indecisively in his hands, as if he did not really know whether to make a fight of it or surrender. Katukov made up his mind for him. His pistol cracked again. The NCO sat down abruptly, rocking back and forth, his shattered kneecap cradled in both hands like a mother comforting a sick child. Katukov sprang over him and wrenched open the door.

A fat officer with an open tunic cowered at the far end of the room, his meal still steaming on the table, a stained napkin tucked into his collarless shirt. It could be no other than the commander of the little force defending the bridge. Calmly Katukov walked over to the plate and taking up the chop which lay there, took a large bite of it, then apparently not satisfied with the taste, sprinkled some salt upon it, before saying in his best German, 'You will not be touched if you obey my orders exactly.'

The German swayed and then fainted clean away. Katukov grinned.

He had done it. For better or worse, the bridge at Kalach was in the hands of the gulag rats.

Ten kilometres away, Colonel Harsch, chewing idly on a piece of hardtack smeared with ersatz honey which made up his first meal of that day, snapped to the half-track driver, 'Turn off the engine.'

Obediently the Dutchman did so, although it would be the very devil to start again in this biting cold. Harsch cocked his head to one side and stared at the faint, flickering pink of the horizon. Who could be firing this far behind the front? he asked himself. Unless some damn fool of a Romanian general had ordered a night exercise. It would by typical of those powdered, perfumed fools who simply didn't know how to treat the average, ragged-arsed stubble-hopper.

'*Schto?*' Igor asked, crouched next to him in the half-track.

Harsch picked up his broken sword and then laid it down again. He could hear nothing. 'Night exercise, I think.'

'Enough boom-boom,' Igor said and resumed his chewing of the hardtack.

At the green-glowing controls, the young Dutchman looked enquiringly at Harsch.

Harsch nodded. 'False alarm. Start her up again, cheesehead. My eggs are freezing up rapidly.'

Obediently, the Dutchman did as he was ordered. The engine, surprisingly enough, started at once and hot air wafted into the steel compartment once more. Harsch returned to his iron-hard biscuit and honey. He'd let the men rest a little longer. Then they'd push on again, Another hour and they'd be at the bridge.

Now all was silent again save for the soft ticking of the engines, the wind breathing icily across the limitless steppe and the crunch of the men biting into the biscuits.

CHAPTER 4

Chuikov read the signal while outside the Stalin organs thundered yet again, bringing the bombardment of the German positions at Stalingrad to an end for this particular November day. He looked up and stared momentarily at Commissar Khrushchev with his bald, high pate and Commissar Malenkov, his face like a soft pudding. Hard as he was, he had to force himself to embrace the man every time they met. His nose sank into the political commissar's fat, round face like going into a half-inflated balloon whenever he had to submit to the man's cold, clinging embrace. Then, by way of setting the cat among the pigeons, he passed the message first to Krushchev and not to Georgi Malenkov, who was Stalin's personal watchdog at his HQ. Nikita Khrushchev and he were bitter rivals, and that master of intrigue knew that Malenkov would gladly report any of his mistakes to the dictator in Moscow.

Krushchev read the message slowly, while Malenkov craned to get a look at it over his shoulder. Chuikov, sitting back in his chair, watched both of the politicians to see how they would react. In the room at the back, the two whores still played that damned gramophone of theirs. Chuikov told himself he would have to stop them soon.

'So,' Khrushchev said and handed the message to Malenkov, who did not bother to read it again but instead said in an icy voice, 'Is that all you have to say, comrade?'

Chuikov sat back in his chair and waited for the fur to fly.

'And what do you wish me to say, comrade?'

'Well, there we have the sauce, don't we!' Malenkov's face flushed a hectic, ugly red as it always did when he was angry.

'How? We know now that there are no Fritz troops within the Romanians' area. That is what these gulag rats were sent out to discover. They have completed their mission successfully.'

'Have they?' Malenkov persisted, and Chuikov knew well what he was thinking. The same thought had occurred to him immediately he had read the rest of that damned fool Katukov's message: '*Have seized bridge at K. Intend to hold until link-up takes place.*'

'What does that mean, Malenkov?' Khrushchev asked. He knew that Stalin had not yet forgiven him for the disaster at Kharkov that spring when the Red Army had lost 200,000 troops because he, Khrushchev, had urged Stalin to ignore warnings of disaster and press the assault; all the same, his obstinate peasant nature would not allow him to back off in front of this monstrous bloated pig from Moscow.

Malenkov extended two thick, hairy sausage-like fingers. 'Two things. One, the Fritz interception service might well be attempting to decipher that message at this very moment, and it won't take them very long to discover where the bridge at K is. Then all hell will be let loose there. Two, what if one of those rats lands in German hands? How long do you think it will take them to make him sing like a yellow canary? Not long, I wager. And what then?'

Chuikov thought it was time to intervene. 'I shall tell you, comrades — the Fritzes will know where we intend to attack on the nineteenth.'

'Exactly,' Malenkov said self-righteously and threw back a lock of greasy black hair which always hung down his low brow. 'Our whole plan will be in the bucket then.'

Khrushchev looked worried. Yet like the peasant he was, he could think on his feet; it was an attribute which had saved his life many times in the years since the revolution and one which would make him the master of all Russia in the next ten years. 'Then we must order that fool at Kalach to withdraw immediately,' he snapped.

'I have already attempted to do so, comrades,' Chuikov said.

'*Attempted?*' the two political commissars echoed in surprised unison.

Chuikov nodded a little unhappily. 'My signals office had just started sending when it was hit by a Fritz 88mm shell.' He scratched at his diseased hand, gritting his teeth a little with the pain. 'By the time other operators were able to go on the air to replace them, they couldn't raise Katukov.'

'That could mean that the Fritzes are already on to them,' Malenkov said eagerly.

'It could mean anything,' Chuikov said. 'Maybe he has gone off the air deliberately. Maybe his set has a defect. Maybe the interference in this area plays a role. After all, there are hundreds of radio sets operating here in an area smaller than that of Moscow. As I said, anything could have happened.'

'At all events, Moscow must be informed at once, and that fool colonel of yours must be punished,' Malenkov snapped, angry that the opportunity to blacken Khrushchev as the person responsible for this failure was slipping from his grasp. 'Now we must give Comrade Stalin a chance to make the correct decision before it is too late.'

'Correct decision?' Chuikov asked.

'Yes, what decision?' the other political commissar added his voice to that of the general.

Malenkov smirked at the two of them, glad to be able to score at last. 'The decision whether the whole counter-attack between Serafimovich and Kletskaya should be cancelled or not.

'Well, Boldin?' Katukov demanded, his boots off as he lay on the commandant's bed and sipped his breakfast tea complete with lemon, for an ample store of them had been found in the HQ.

'Everything's running very smoothly,' Boldin reported. 'A bunch of Romanians came through on their *panje*-wagons heading for Stalingrad. A busload of German leave-men, as drunk as howitzers, came the other way heading for the railhead and leave in the fascist homeland.' He shrugged easily. 'So far, so good. Nobody seems to have tumbled to the fact that all is not well at Kalach!' He indicated the window with a jerk of his thumb to the spot where the commandant, dressed in his best uniform, wandered up and down the street, saluting and smirking wildly, knowing that if he pulled any tricks, Glinka, hidden in the HQ's look-out tower, would blow his brains out with his rifle. 'And our tame Fritz is doing very well. He must have been in the theatre.'

Katukov nodded his agreement. 'You see, my dear Boldin, my plan did work out well after all. Now they know the situation at Stalingrad, and I'm sure the commanding general is very glad to have this little Trojan Horse planted firmly at a key spot in the Fritz positions. It will be useful, very useful, later on.'

'Perhaps,' Boldin answered noncommittally, 'though I wish we were still in radio communication with Stalingrad. Who would have thought that that long-nosed German bastard would pull a trick like that, knocking out our radio operator and destroying the radio? Ah well, he's one Fritz less to worry us.'

Katukov's smile vanished. 'Yes, Boldin, and that fool out there assures me that they did not have to report in by radio to their authorities or anything like that. So the failure of radio contact is no problem as far as the Germans are concerned.'

'All the same,' Boldin said, 'I'd like to know what our people are doing. There is —' He stopped abruptly.

'What's the matter?' Katukov asked, sitting up suddenly.

Boldin didn't answer. Instead, he hurried to the window.

The commandant had stopped his posturing and was standing in the centre of the snow-covered street, hand half-raised to his cap, staring up to the bridge where the gunners were hurrying to their positions on the flak cannon.

'*Shit, thrice-times shit!*' Boldin cursed.

And this time Katukov, hastening towards him, did not need to ask why his second-in-command had cursed. There was no mistaking that squeaky, rusty rattle. Armoured vehicles were approaching the bridge from the other side of the Don — and they could only be enemy ones.

Colonel Harsch cursed the Dutch driver who had stalled the command half-track just as it had begun to take the climb that led to the bridge. The damned cheesehead had failed to change down in time and the engine had refused to take the strain in a too-high gear. Now the blonde-headed driver swore, red-faced, at the ignition, while a grinning Duclos in the medic half-track rattled by them on his way to the bridge. 'Heaven, arse and cloudburst, man!' Harsch roared and slapped his sword against the steel side of the vehicle. 'For God's sake, sort it out!'

Angrily Harsch dropped over the side and stared up the road towards Kalach. His next half-track came roaring round the bend, its driver ramming home low gear, the troopers packing its deck grinning at their commander's discomfiture. Suddenly

Harsch forgot his anger as his gaze fell on the commandant whom they had met briefly on their way into the Don Basin.

The man was striding up and down the street like a damned wooden puppet saluting briskly to left and right, saluting even before the slovenly clad soldiers raised their hands in greeting to him. There was something else strange about Kalach and its defenders. All of the soldiers wore the precious Russian *valenki*, the felt-lined boots of the Red Army which were so greedily sought after by the German *Landser*, where had these rear-echelon stallions obtained them? In his own command only a quarter of his men had them. What was going on in Kalach?

Suddenly Harsch made a decision. He sprang into the middle of the road, sword upraised.

Groetjean, the big Flemish driver of the leading half-track, hit the brakes hard. The carrier shuddered to a stop only a metre away from the lean figure of the CO, almost skidding into the ditch on the frozen snow. Behind it the others rolled to a stop. Now the only vehicle moving was that of Duclos, clattering over the metal bridge in low gear getting ever closer to the suddenly stationary soldiers on the other side and the fat fool of a commandant poised there with his pudgy fist half-raised to his cap saluting nobody like an absurd waxwork figure…

'*They know!*' Boldin said grimly, lowering his glasses.

Next to him, Katukov took his eyes off that lean, handsome young German standing in the middle of the road, what looked like a broken sword in his one hand, and knew Boldin was right. '*Damn, damn, damn!*' he cursed. For a moment or two he was too paralysed to act, but then Boldin's urgent question made him realize the urgency of their situation. 'Do?' he echoed Boldin's query. 'They're stalled on that road! Quick! To those two flak guns down there. At that range, we might have a chance to knock them out. Come on, Boldin!'

Frantically, the two officers clattered down the stairs from their observation post in the HQ tower, scattering astonished rats as they ran, crying to the gunners, who were not yet properly awake. 'Fire ... fire at the Fritz bastards. *Fire!*'

'*Duclos!*' Harsch yelled as he saw the men rushing for the twin flak guns at the far side of the river and knew instinctively what was going to happen. 'In God's name, reverse ... *reverse!*' But Duclos, unable to hear above the roar of the tracks as the half-track clattered ever closer to the other side, just smiled and waved.

The doctor was twenty metres away when the frantic gunners at the first flak cannon finally brought down their twin-barrelled weapon to ground level and Duclos's driver realized that something was wrong. He slammed on the brakes. Duclos, taken by surprise, slapped against the cab. The driver rammed home reverse, just as the first wild slugs from Kalach came howling off the steel plating. Duclos saw their danger. He seized the cab machine-gun and swung it from left to right, scything down running men everywhere, while the driver started to roll backwards, the half-track zigzagging from left to right.

'Come on, come on!' Harsch cried in frenzied excitement, gripping the sword in a white-knuckled hand. 'Come on, you bastard, get back ... *get back!*'

The flack gun opened up with an hysterical screech. White, glowing 200mm shells hissed through the air by the hundred. The half-track reeled under the impact. Great gleaming silver holes appeared abruptly along its length. White smoke started to pour from the shattered engine. Still, somehow, it continued to roll backwards, the dying, blinded driver jerking the wheel back and forth, the strength ebbing out of him, as if a tap had been opened.

Now the crippled half-track was only a matter of metres from Harsch's end of the bridge. They were going to do it, he told himself, as behind him the rest of the *Kampfgruppe* started to scuttle backwards to the safety of the bend, their machine-gunners sending streams of red and white tracer hissing across the Don at the men on the other side.

With a resounding crash the half-track slid, suddenly completely out of control, across the bridge and buried its blunt snout in a heap of brick rubble.

Harsch groaned. They hadn't a chance now. Two flak guns concentrated their cruel fire on the crippled half-track. It disappeared under a hail of flying white shells. Harsch beat his sword against the side of his own vehicle in blind rage, then he, too, was swinging himself over the side as the flak cannon turned their fire on the last half-track.

The battle for the bridge at Kalach had commenced.

CHAPTER 5

The half-track crept slowly up the narrow winding path that led from the river towards the stark black outline of the trees, tinged every now and again by silver when the moon appeared from behind the scudding clouds. Behind them on the other side of the Don there was the faint rattle of Harsch's own vehicles, the three half-tracks of the HQ group, as they made their way to the cover of the forest in which they would hide till dawn.

Goldwasser scanned his front carefully and then whispered to the French driver, '*allez* — *advance!*'

The young Parisian gunned his motor — unnecessarily loudly in Goldwasser's opinion — and then took the incline. A moment later they were on the river road heading straight for Kalach, with Goldwasser asking himself whether or not he had been a damn fool to have volunteered for this dangerous mission. Naturally it had been his idea to float a half-track across the Don way down below the bridge, out of earshot and sight of the Reds. Harsch, the one-armed German, had called his idea 'kapital' and had slapped him on the back exuberantly, saying, 'Well, Goldwasser, I can tell I've got a Jew in the Fire Brigade now. They always come up with something!'

Perhaps it had been that which had prompted him to say, 'With your permission, *Obersturmbannführer*, I should like to take charge of the mission.' Here he was, a Jew, leading a dozen young cut-throats from all over Europe, who were the sworn enemies of his race. If he had not been too scared to consider the situation, he would have found it ironic.

Harsch had been able to see the irony of his position — a Jew in charge of a dozen SS men. His parting words had been, as his men had towed the rough-and-ready float back across the Don by means of a rope, 'Bring me back one prisoner, Goldwasser, and I'll apply to *Reichsführer* Himmler for permission for you to join the Black Guards. Hell, we might even form a Jewish Brigade!' And roaring with laughter at his own cynical humour, Harsch had staggered back to the trees where he and his group would hide.

Now they were on their way and once again Goldwasser ran his mind over the details of the plan which should bag them the prisoner whom Harsch needed to find out the details of the Reds' mission in the Don Basin. To the east of the bridge on the road they were presently taking was an isolated *isba*, which housed, or so it appeared from Harsch's study of the place through his binoculars that afternoon, a company HQ or something of that sort. With a bit of luck they would be able to surprise the staff housed there, pick up the most senior officer present and be off with him before the Reds had woken up to what was happening. At least that was the plan, but as Goldwasser told himself with a certain sinking feeling, in the Alpini they had always maintained that a plan was like a horse designed by a committee — it always turned out to be a camel!

Captain Simonvitch sniffed the night air and told himself it was going to snow. Somewhere a wolf howled at the sickle-moon. But Simonvitch did not hear it; his mind was too occupied with the state of his company. That afternoon, after a tally of the stores found in the captured village, Colonel Katukov had ordered that from now onwards until they were finally relieved by the great counter-attack, there would be a ration of 400 grams of bread, a canteen of oats to cook their *kavka* and 100 grams of salt pork per day. It did not seem much to feed the hungry men of his command, and besides, as he had explained to Katukov, 'My men need greens or something containing vitamin C. Otherwise they'll get scurvy and their teeth will fall out.'

Katukov had replied with a coarse laugh, 'Then they won't be able to eat so much hard-tack, and the ration'll go further!'

Simonvitch shrugged. People like Katukov simply didn't realize that soldiers were just like schoolchildren; one had to be fussing after them all the time or they'd get into trouble. Then hitching up his pistol-belt and forgetting the matter, he began his nightly round of the company sentries, the only company commander in the 333rd Punishment Battalion who would leave the roaring comfort of the great green-tiled ovens of the *isbas* to do so on such a cold night.

The Frenchman turned off the half-track's engine and now all was silence save for the howl of the wind in the trees in which they had hidden the vehicle.

'Do you think you'll be able to get it started again when we're back here?' Goldwasser asked a little anxiously.

'*Bien sûr*,' the driver said. '*Regardez!*' From behind his seat he brought out a small can, punctured with holes and half-filled with earth. Taking a jerrican, he carefully poured about a litre of precious gasoline into the earth and with his bayonet began to stir the mixture into a thick goo, while Goldwasser watched puzzled. Finally, he achieved the right consistency and shoved the can underneath the half-track's engine. He scratched a match and threw it into the can. It ignited at once and soft blue flames started to flicker upwards. 'Dangerous,' he said in accented German, 'but effective.'

Goldwasser shook his head in admiration. These young toughs in whose company he now found himself seemed to be able to master every situation; he would never have dreamed of trying to keep a motor ready to start in that manner.

Five minutes later the little group of SS men were nearing the edge of the village, stealing from shadow to shadow, the only sound being the soft squeak of their own sock-covered boots on the frozen snow, the wind drowning whatever noise that came from the darkened huts. Nothing stirred. They could not even detect a sentry. It seemed as if the plan was going to work without trouble. Silently Goldwasser, the lead, said a prayer that it would.

'Sentry,' hissed one of the SS men to the right of Goldwasser.

The rest froze into immobility. Goldwasser heard his heart thumping away like the brass band of the Alpini on revue day in front of the King and Il Duce. 'Where?' he asked in a thin, strangled voice.

'There, somewhere,' the soldier whispered back, 'I can hear the red pig snoring.'

'What are we going to do?' Goldwasser asked a little helplessly.

'Take him,' the man who had reported the sentry hissed. 'Leave it to me, lieutenant.'

Cautiously hugging the silver shadows, the little patrol advanced towards the sound of the snoring, their boots making hardly a sound. Twenty metres … fifteen … ten … five. Abruptly the snoring ceased. Goldwasser felt a shiver of fear run down his spine. The sentry was waking up!

They froze. Before them they could make out the man, a bearded Russian, with his rifle clasped between his arms, as if he were cradling a precious child. The sentry opened his eyes.

They could hear him yawn. Then he saw them, the men crouching there in the shadows who had not been there when he had gone to sleep. They heard his sharp intake of breath. In an instant he would shout out.

'Get him!' Goldwasser heard himself hiss.

Two of the SS men shot forward. One of them smashed the side of his hand against the man's mouth.

The other kneed him cruelly. The sentry's breath fled from him in an anguished gasp. He started to fall forward. His helmet tumbled to the ground, Goldwasser caught it in the very last moment. As the sentry's bent neck lurched past him, the first SS man brought his clenched fist down in a brutal blow. The Russian hit the snow, unconscious, just as Captain Simonvitch came round the corner doing his rounds with his stupidly cheerful, 'Damnable cold tonight, sentry, wh —' He took in the situation at once. '*Alarm, alarm —*'

Instinctively Goldwasser pressed the trigger of his pistol. Simonvitch's cry of warning ended in a scream of pain as the slug smashed into his chest. He went reeling back, clutching the wound with wet, red fingers.

The Frenchman, sweating and cursing, drove the ten-ton monster as if he were back at the wheel of the taxi he had had in Paris before the war. He swung the half-track's wheel back and forth, while the tracer zipped through the air lethally, and over at the bridge, the Russians loosed salvo after salvo after the fleeing raiders.

They smashed through a fence. A group of Russians skidded like ice-skaters to a stop in front of them. Immediately they crouched and began firing. Standing up on the deck one of the SS men fanned the air with his hands and plunged down dead on his comrades. Another lobbed a stick grenade at the Russians. They flew apart and the half-track rattled on.

'*Savoia!*' Goldwasser cried, yelling out the battle-cry of the Alpini, carried away by the wild excitement of this strange chase in the middle of the night.

A flare exploded in a blinding flash of brilliant white light to their front. Unable to see for an instant, the driver smashed into a small thatched-roof hut. With a burst of crashing glass, they were through, the bullets howling angrily off their metal sides. A second later the roof collapsed with a thunderous roar. 'Shit, driver,' one of the SS men yelled above the rattling tracks and snap-and-crackle of small-arms fire, 'what's this — a bleeding mystery tour!'

The sweating Frenchman took his hands off the wheel for a moment, 'You can drive it if you like, cheesehead!'

'No, no!' the cries of protest came from all sides.

'*Sales cons,*' the Frenchman cursed to himself and concentrated on driving again.

They shot through a small garden, smashed down the picket fence on the other side, and swerved into a narrow, tree-lined lane. A Russian loomed up out of the trees. Before anyone could stop him, he lobbed a grenade into the half-track. It exploded with a tremendous impact in those confined quarters. Goldwasser heard the shrapnel hissing through the air all round him. Men screamed and went down everywhere. Then they were out of the lane and a terrified Goldwasser recognized the road they had come in on. 'To the right, driver!' he screamed. '*A droit.*'

'*Merde!*' the Frenchman cried and swung the wheel round violently.

A bunch of squat Russian infantry sprang up from the ditch. Goldwasser swung his machine-gun from left to right.

Gasping, he scythed them down, bowling their bodies to left and right as if they were puppets at the hands of a crazed puppet-master.

They were through. Crazily they rattled into the darkness, bearing with them a cargo of dead and dying in the blood-filled back of the half-track — and the vital prisoner.

CHAPTER 6

'You can go — he'll survive.' With his broken sword, Harsch waved away the medical orderly who had been patching up the wound in Simonvitch's shoulder. He examined his prisoner for the first time, noting that the small, skinny man bore only the insignia of an officer, but otherwise no means of identification. Harsch indicated that Goldwasser should hand the Russian the bottle of *Moskovskaya* vodka, which stood on the ration crate.

Simonvitch nodded and took a hearty gulp of the fiery vodka. Harsch considered the fact. Probably a former political prisoner, he told himself, and some sort of intellectual to boot to judge by the fact he understood German. It should make his task easier; that type broke quickly.

'All right, that's enough,' he commanded and Simonvitch handed the bottle back to Goldwasser, staring up at the handsome blonde SS officer with frightened, short-sighted eyes. 'Now then, captain. I want to ask you two or three simple questions. Answer them quickly and I promise you that I'll have you in the nearest Romanian hospital for proper treatment for your wound.'

'What sort of questions?' the prisoner asked hesitantly in German, his accent strangely familiar to Harsch, though at that moment he couldn't place it.

Harsch smiled at him. With the Russians, he knew, once they began talking they usually continued to do so. This one had started. 'First, your unit.'

'The 333rd Punishment Battalion,' Simonvitch answered, staring at his felt boots.

'Ah, the redoubtable gulag rats,' Harsch said. 'I've heard of you. From the concentration camps, aren't you? And yet heroes of the Soviet paradise, always ready to sacrifice your lives for the little Father up there in the Kremlin who sent you to them in the first place. Very curious.' He swung his broken sword, while Simonvitch remained silent. 'Second question. Why did you take the bridge at Kalach?'

Again Simonvitch answered the question without taking his gaze from his boots. 'Because our fool of a colonel ordered us to.'

Harsch grinned. 'It is common in all armies, Ivan,' he said and winked at Goldwasser. 'We are all led by fools. But that isn't exactly the answer I wanted. Perhaps I should phrase my question differently. What was the mission of your battalion so deep behind Romanian lines?' For the first time the prisoner did not answer. Instead he looked up from his boots, first at the handsome German and then at the dark-faced, hooked-nosed Italian, allowing his gaze to rest on the Alpini officer's face as if the look had some significance. Goldwasser dropped his gaze, oddly embarrassed.

Harsch gripped his sword more firmly and pressed the broken blade against the Russian's arm — hard. Simonvitch screamed. Blood began to trickle through the thick serge of his blouse. He stared down at it aghast. 'I asked you a question, Ivan,' Harsch said as calm as ever, while Goldwasser licked suddenly dry lips.

'I'm not answering,' Simonvitch said, his shortsighted eyes liquid with tears.

'It has cost me eight good men to capture you for the answer to that question,' Harsch said evenly. 'I'm not going to allow you to deny me it.'

'You can do what you like,' Simonvitch said, trying to keep his voice level. 'But I won't speak.'

'I wonder ... I wonder.' Harsch raised his voice, 'Igor, take your countryman outside and let him have a little think about his decision.'

Igor spat on the floor of the tent. '*Buka!*' he cursed, and pushed Simonvitch in front of him.

The prisoner flung a last glance at the two officers. '*Nuzi smerti, nye budet,*' he snarled and went.

'What did he say?' Goldwasser asked, worried by the turn of events.

Harsch laughed. 'It can't be worse than death. A vain hope I am afraid, *teniente*. It is.'

'What?' Goldwasser said, already knowing what the answer to that question would be.

'Torture!'

'You couldn't!'

'Of course, I could — and *can*.' Harsch looked down at him. '*Mein lieber* Goldwasser, we're in Russia, not the Vatican City. We torture, they torture. It is a way of life out here in this God-forsaken wasteland.' He smiled a little grimly. 'My grandfather and my father would have been horrified, but then they did not have to serve a Hitler or fight a Stalin. Times have changed and the customs of war, too.' He sniffed. 'Besides, your own Duce is not averse to using the rubber truncheon and somewhat large doses of castor oil to get information out of his prisoners, they tell me, eh?'

Goldwasser said nothing and Harsch clapped him on the back. 'Don't take it to heart, old fellow. We'll have that Ivan singing like a canary before the hour is out.' But there *Obersturmbannführer* Harsch was wrong for once.

Five kilometres away at the other side of the river, the winter dawn came slowly, as if reluctant to throw its warming light on the war-torn countryside, Boldin and Katukov surveyed the situation and took stock of their assets.

Together they watched for a while as the gulag rats collected the dead of the night's raid and carried them to the river where the fast flowing water soon bore away the bodies; the earth was too hard to dig graves and both officers knew the men would soon need all their strength for other and more important things. Then Katukov took Boldin's arm and led him away so that they were out of earshot of the soldiers. 'He'll talk, I suppose, Boldin,' he said.

Boldin knew immediately to whom the colonel referred. 'He's a bit of an old woman, typical schoolteacher, comrade colonel, but he's tough all the same.'

'But he'll talk,' Katukov persisted.

Boldin nodded. 'We all do in the end.'

'So that alters our situation somewhat, doesn't it?'

'Yes.' Boldin looked across the river, the fog drifting away from its surface now in ghostly wreaths, as if he half-expected to see infantry already there.

'What do you think will happen?' Katukov asked. 'They'll bring up infantry, of course,' Boldin said coolly as if they were back at staff college and they were discussing some sand-table tactical problem. 'If they can get the Romanians to co-ordinate correctly with them, they'll put in an attack from both flanks simultaneously. But naturally that won't happen straightaway. The way the Romanians move, I'd give them another twenty-four hours. Dawn tomorrow morning is my guess.'

'Mine, too, Boldin,' Katukov agreed. 'But before then we can expect enemy air attacks. Dive-bombers, probably. They won't want to destroy the bridge itself if they can help it, but they'll want to soften us up for the infantry attack.'

'Yes.' Boldin looked at his watch. It was nearly seven. The sky was beginning to brighten more rapidly, illuminating the shell-stripped trees along the river bank so that they looked like gaunt outsize toothpicks. 'By the time Simonvitch spills the beans and higher headquarters has been informed, it will be midday. The fly-boys won't want to miss their precious lunch, so it could be at least two o'clock before they're airborne on their way here. Just time to give us thirty minutes of their steel eggs before it grows too hazy — and back to the mess for English high tea, complete with serviettes.'

'Don't be so damned frivolous! The situation is very serious, Boldin, you know.'

'I know, comrade colonel,' Boldin answered cheerfully. 'But life is far too serious to be taken seriously, they always say.' The smile vanished from his tough face and he was very businesslike. 'Where do we establish our positions, comrade colonel?'

'*Madre de dio!*' Goldwasser exclaimed in horror.

The Russian prisoner's naked body was smeared with blood, both eyes were almost closed, his face a mass of black swollen bruises and his right kneecap showed white through the black caked blood of the open wound there.

Simonvitch flicked open his eyes and was aware again that he had talked. The squat Igor who had done the torturing had finally broken him. He had talked, then fallen into unconsciousness.

Now he awoke with that terrible betrayal uppermost in his mind. And he was dying and knew it.

'*Zhid?*' he asked in Russian through cracked, bloodied lips. '*Zhid?*'

Goldwasser swallowed hard and, looking down at the Russian's tortured body, saw that he was indeed circumcised; that had been the reason for that significant look before the torture had commenced. 'Yes,' he said softly, 'I'm a Jew too.'

Simonvitch attempted a smile and failed miserably. With a weak wave of his hand, he indicated that Goldwasser should come closer.

The Italian officer did so. 'What do you want?' he asked.

'Pistol,' Simonvitch croaked. 'Jew, give me your pistol...' He put his forefinger weakly to his forehead and made the motion of pulling a trigger. 'No, brother, you ... you shoot me.'

Goldwasser recoiled with horror. 'Kill you!' he exclaimed. 'I couldn't ... no, I couldn't do that!'

'Brother, you must!' Simonvitch, his eyes flickering wildly, clutched Goldwasser's hand. '*Palshalsta* ... please.'

'No, no,' Goldwasser said, 'I couldn't, even if you are a Jew, too. I simply couldn't!'

'Then I will.'

It was Colonel Harsch standing there at the entrance to the tent, sword tucked into his belt, his one hand hovering at his pistol holster.

'You?'

'Yes, why not. One has to be in good shape to commit suicide, you know? The little fellow was brave, but in the end he talked.' He shrugged. 'It was to be expected.'

'Shoot!' the man on the floor croaked piteously, arms extended in a gesture of supplication.

'Oh, my God, I can't stand this!' It took Goldwasser all his will-power not to break down and cry. Blindly he blundered by the tall blonde SS officer into the cold air.

An instant later a single shot rang out and Harsch left the tent, placing his pistol back into his holster a little awkwardly. 'I don't know what you Jews say over your dead,' he said gruffly. 'But he was a brave little bastard, so say something.'

Without another look at Goldwasser he strode away and began to stare purposefully at the sky for the planes which would soon come...

CHAPTER 7

Nothing!

Nothing happened. Neither the infantry nor the expected dive-bombers arrived at the bridge at Kalach. The gulag rats extended their positions into the apple orchard to the east of the bridge, piling the snow up high, urinating over the cracks before smoothing them with their entrenching tools so that the frost would turn the snow into impenetrable ice. Boldin and Katukov surveyed the hundred-metre-high bluff on the western side from which had come the rattle of the German half-tracks. But nothing stirred there. An uneasy quiet had descended upon that part of the steppe. '*Boshe moi!*' Boldin cursed, lowering his glasses and blowing on his frozen fingers, 'you would think that the damned war had gone home and got into bed.'

And as the hours crept by with no sign of the Germans preparing for an attack, Colonel Katukov could only agree with him.

Half a kilometre away, huddled in the freezing tent together with Goldwasser, a moody Harsch was asking himself the same question that puzzled the officers of the 333rd Punishment Battalion: *what was going on?*

With Operation Uranus less than six days away, Josef Stalin had suddenly got cold feet. Malenkov's message had broken his confidence in the success of the flank attack. Behind the blacked-out windows in his Kremlin apartment, he paced the floor in his high boots, alternatively sucking his curved pipe and running its mouthpiece through his drooping, dyed moustache while barrel-chested Marshal Zhukov, his chief military adviser, watched him helplessly.

Stalin paused only to moan, 'Now the Fritzes'll know everything ... *everything*, Zhukov!'

Inwardly Zhukov cursed the damned obscure colonel and his gulag scum who had captured the bridge and caused all this fuss, but outwardly he maintained an air of impressive calm, knowing it would be up to him to somehow convince the dictator that all was well. Nothing, not even foreknowledge of the offensive, could prevent it being successful now. All that long evening he had worked on Stalin, giving him a controlled, dispassionate recital of the facts: the thousands of tanks that made up the Russian Fifth and Twenty-first Tank Armies, the 3500 guns which would herald the attack with an hour-long bombardment of the Romanian positions, the hundreds of thousands of infantrymen ready to follow up the armoured breakthrough. But still the dictator remained unconvinced, knowing that if he failed this time it might well mean the end of his regime.

Two thousand kilometres away at his mountain retreat, the Berghof, in the snow-bound Bavarian Alps, Hitler also remained strangely inactive, in spite of the warnings that had now reached him of the Russians' intentions. He dallied with his mistress Eva Braun, enjoyed his peppermint tea and cream cakes in front of the huge blazing fire, and whiled away the long evenings listening to Wagner and Lehar on the gramophone, expounding his theories to the toadying Borman and the rest of his cronies on everything from the superiority of the baked potato over the boiled one, to the inability of the average French woman to produce a boy child suitable for the infantry.

Hitler that November seemed strangely settled, already beginning to make plans for his future life in peacetime. For he was convinced the great Reich he had created in the last three years would endure. Did not his armies rule over 300 million people and over territory stretching from the French Atlantic coastline to the foothills of the Caucasus, and from the northern capes of Norway down to the yellow sands of Libya? Occasionally his military staff managed to get him into the conference room and attempt to explain the true state of affairs on the Don, but Hitler did not seem really interested by the threat to the Romanian and, of course, Paulus's Sixth Armies. He would peer at the maps through his steel-rimmed spectacles, ask the usual questions about the weather and what Luftwaffe groups were operating in the Stalingrad area. But otherwise he did nothing.

He had reached the zenith of his power. In his fanatical heart he was convinced that nothing could dethrone him now.

It was while the generals, both German and Russian, waited in this strange hiatus, knowing what should be done, but with their hands tied by their political masters, that a very slight, very pale civilian presented himself at Chuikov's underground headquarters and asked politely if he could see the general.

The elegant staff officers lounging at the door of the tunnel, enjoying a minute's rest from the strain of directing the battle which still raged in the ruins of Stalingrad, laughed in the little civilian's face and told him this day Chuikov wasn't even seeing full generals; he had too much on his plate. That was until the civilian pulled out his NKVD identity card with the six letters written in bold red underneath the photograph, 'S-M-E-R-S-H'.

'*Smersh!*' the senior man exclaimed, his ruddy face suddenly pale and frightened. It was the first time he had ever met a member of that organization dreaded throughout the Soviet Union, but like everyone else in Russia he had heard of it. Hurriedly he strode into the HQ tunnel. One minute later, General Chuikov was facing the little civilian, studying the man while he waited for him to state his reason for appearing so strangely in the middle of a battlefield.

The civilian had straight, lustreless black hair, the high bony forehead of an intellectual and flat, dark, impenetrable eyes. His eyes together with the pencil-thin black moustache which came down below his cruel-lipped mouth gave him an almost oriental appearance. But it was his hands that caught Chuikov's attention. They didn't seem to belong to that skinny, slight body: they were monstrous things, heavy-knuckled and covered with thick black hairs, and they hung almost to the man's knees when he stood up. They were apelike and frightening; the hands of a killer. The man from Smersh smiled suddenly and an instant later it was as if he had never smiled in all his life. 'I suppose you are wondering, general,' he said in a dull, but somehow ironic voice, 'what I am doing here in this place?'

'Yes, I am somewhat,' Chuikov answered uneasily, scratching frantically at his bandaged fingers wet with the sticky moisture of his weeping eczema.

'It is concerning this — er — Colonel Katukov.' His eyes looked at Chuikov lifelessly above that trick moustache, as if he were not really interested in the Hero of Stalingrad, just his own words, which had to be selected with great care. 'I would be grateful if you could let me have the latest information you have on him and his battalion.' Inwardly Chuikov breathed a sigh of relief. At least the matter had nothing directly to do with him. 'There's nothing much I can tell you, comrade —' he hesitated, but the man from Smersh did not supply his name, 'except that he disobeyed orders by taking the bridge at Kalach. We have reason to believe that the Fritzes already know what his mission is, due to this vain-glorious foolishness. But they have not yet acted —'

The man from Smersh held up his hand and Chuikov stopped speaking immediately, as if he were a simple soldier and not a full general of the Red Army.

'I'm not interested in the larger issues, just the situation at the bridge, general.'

'I see,' Chuikov said hastily, though he didn't.

'How far is this bridge at Kalach from here?'

'Three … four hours,' Chuikov hazarded a guess. 'But why?'

The man from Smersh poked one of his monstrous hands at his eye and rubbed the eyeball as if he were tired. 'You will supply me with a troop of your best commandos,' he said, not answering Chuikov's question directly, but then the men of Smersh never felt constrained to answer anyone's questions, however highly placed that individual might be, save perhaps those of Beria, and he, too, if the rumour were true, was a little afraid of his Smersh operatives. They will slip me through the Fritz lines and turn back.'

'Slip you through the Fritz lines!' Chuikov exclaimed incredulously. 'But what … what to do?' He looked in red-faced amazement at the slight civilian.

The man from Smersh tittered; it was a strange, uncanny sound at that moment, and it made the small hairs at the back of Chuikov's neck stand erect with fear. 'Nothing very much, comrade general. Just to do my duty as a Smersh operative.' His voice hardened suddenly and his dark eyes gleamed. 'I'll just kill the bastard, that's all…'

CHAPTER 8

In the thin yellow November sunshine, Corporal Glinka delicately picked the lice out of the seams of his grey Wehrmacht shirt and laid them on the barrel of the flak cannon, only half listening to Sergeant Sviechka's account of his last encounter with a female before he had been sent to the camps in 1939. 'Well, I managed to get her arse-curtains off without too much trouble,' the bearded NCO with the cross-eyes was saying, 'and of course, yer must remember in them days they had really frilly ones, with lace and everythin'.'

'Shut up, sergeant,' one of his listeners protested in a high mock falsetto, 'you'll have me coming down my leg in half a minute, you dog!'

The other members of the gun crew laughed softly, enjoying the sun, the story, this time out of war. Glinka placed another dead louse on the barrel and said, 'Sleep tight, my little German louse. Your Hitler will pray for you, now you have fallen for Fatherland and Führer.'

'But then the trouble started when I tried to cock my leg over her hams and mount her,' Sviechka continued. '"You mustn't", she cried. "I must conserve my strength for Stalin and the completion of the Five-Year Plan. What would the Little Father say?"'

The others rocked with laughter at the bearded sergeant's imitation of the unknown woman in that peacetime wheatfield so long ago.

'So I said to her in anger, "Didn't you know that your 'Little Father' fucks little boys?" Oh, did that do it! Up she was in a flash, frilly knickers in her hand, running through the corn, her skirt up in her haste showing all her arse — and I must admit comrades, it was a big one, as big as any hundred rouble mare, and then, was the watch in the bucket! A couple of thousand Greenhats jumped on me, pounded my butt into the shit with their clubs and hauled me away in chains. Next day the NKVD magistrate sentenced me to twenty-five years in the gulag… Wait for it, comrades,' he held up his big horny hand. 'Not for what you think, but for sabotaging the Five-Year Plan!'

The others expressed their disbelief, as Sergeant Sviechka anticipated they would.

'Yes. Apparently my remark sent the bitch into such a state that she couldn't drive the combined harvester that summer so that made it a serious case of economic sabotage. Hence the twenty-five years.'

He sniffed and tugged the end of his stub-nose. 'The last I heard of the big mare, she was running a Fritz brothel — for their officers who fancied little boys. So much for Stalin's loyal virgin.'

They laughed again and Glinka raised his head from the lice-hunt to say mockingly, 'Come off it, Yuri, everybody knows you only like sheep.'

Once more the men laughed and Sergeant Sviechka said coarsely, '*Job tvojemat!*'

'Can't, Yuri,' Glinka said easily, 'she's had a Moscow metro train up there these —' He stopped suddenly and looked upwards.

The others heard the noise at the very same instant. All eyes swung to the winter sky. And there they were. Three Stukas hovering above the bridge like great sinister crows. The Fritzes had begun to react at last.

'Now listen you pomaded warm-brother of a flyboy,' Harsch said over the field telephone. 'I want your boys up there at the double and give the Ivans a taste of your square eggs.'

At the other end of the line, his cousin, *Geschwader-kommodore* Ritter von Heide, commander of the Richthofen Wing, tut-tutted in that affected manner of his, and at that moment Harsch could imagine him screwing the monocle, which he didn't need, a little more firmly into his pale yellow eye. He then replied, 'But my dear crippled fellow, one can't go around starting private wars like this. Fat Hermann wouldn't take kindly to it one little bit.'

'*Quelle horreur*! One can't speak like that about our illustrious commander, *Reichsmarschall* Hermann Göring.'

'He can go and shit in his field-marshal's hat'.

'Tut-tut, this present unpleasantness has really coarsened you. I do declare that you'll never be received in a Berlin *salon* again. Your language is frightfully coarse. That comes of joining such a working-class unit as the armed SS!'

'Stick your salami in yer own rear entrance and give yourself a cheap thrill.'

Von Heide gave a whimper of delight. 'I say, old chap, you are really surpassing yourself. That's a good one! Can I use it?'

Harsch grinned. His horse-faced affected cousin was a card. 'You may. Now what about a few Stukas?'

'What's it worth to you, cousin? If I'm going to get myself put up against the nearest wall when this business comes out and have my turnip shot off, I want to know that it was worth it.'

'Champagne?' Harsch suggested.

'How much and what quality?' von Heide snapped quickly and Harsch could almost scent his greed over the field telephone.

'A case for every Stuka crew. A case for you, naturally. Brut ... Château Rothschild.'

'*Zucker!*' his cousin breathed over the field telephone. 'A dream, though one would hate to think what the Führer would say — a Jewish champagne, what next?'

'He'll never know. If you have inhibitions, send him some regulation-issue peppermint tea to brighten his miserable existence.'

'Enough, enough treacherous talk,' Ritter von Heide said hastily. 'Walls have ears you know. What do you want?'

'I have a nice little bunch of Popov's trapped down here at Kalach, a hundred kilometres or more behind our own lines. But seemingly nobody wants to know of their existence. So, as I said earlier on, I've decided to start a small private war with them. For it, I need your daring young flyboys in their Stukas to give me cover when I cross the Don.'

'I see.' His cousin absorbed the information and then said, 'You did say Brut ... Château Rothschild?'

'I did indeed.'

'Good, then you've got your Stukas. Over and out!'

'Over and out!' Harsch echoed, a smile on his lips, asking himself if wars had always been fought like this. A minute later he decided they had.

'*Alarm ... alarm...*'

The cries ran from man to man. NCO's shrilled their whistles. Officers shouted commands while above them the three black-painted Stukas hovered, above the running men like great sinister hawks.

Abruptly, as Sergeant Sviechka's flak-cannon started to pump a white glowing stream of 20mm shells into the sky, the flight-leader flung himself out of the sky. Hurtling downwards, sirens screaming hideously, engine howling in wild protest, the Stuka came straight down at a lunatic speed, the flak flashing by it and exploding in little balls of brown cotton wool. On and on it came. Would it never pull out of that crazy dive?

Just when it seemed the Fritz had to crash into the bridge, the pilot jerked back the stick. The Stuka seemed to stop in mid-air. Later Glinka would swear he had seen the rivets falling off the dive-bomber as its fuselage shuddered and trembled under that tremendous strain. Suddenly a myriad deadly black eggs tumbled rapidly from its sky-blue belly and hurtled to the ground. A pattern of explosions rippled along the snow-covered fields on both sides of the bridge, appearing brown against the white, like the work of a gigantic mole. Fist-sized, red-hot chunks of metal whizzed everywhere. Next to Glinka on the chattering flak-gun, Sergeant Sviechka howled in agony. Glinka, his brow wet with sweat, glanced over at him. Yuri's bearded face seemed to be slipping slowly down to his chest like molten wax, leaving behind a noseless, eyeless, gory red something. Without another word, Yuri fell to the ground — dead.

But Glinka had no time to worry about his running-mate now. The second German was coming down at 400 kilometres an hour. Hurriedly he pressed his eye to the sight again. The twin barrels began to chatter furiously once more. The sky all around the black, diving plane was peppered brown. Still it came on. Again the whole world seemed dominated by that ear-splitting, terrifying scream of the Stuka's twin sirens, followed a moment later by the howl of the air brakes as the pilot wrenched the plane out its dive and the hundred-pound bombs whistled down on the gulag rats' positions.

This time the German was more accurate. The bombs straddled the orchard positions, smashing into the ice strongpoints, flinging dead and dying rats on all sides. High above the battlefield, the flight-leader watched the destruction with pleasure and told himself he'd earned his case of 'frog lemonade'.

Now the last plane came hurtling down. But he was not to be as fortunate as his fellows. On all sides machine-gun and flak fire concentrated on the lone German, white curving tracer filling the air like thick flying hail.

Suddenly the Stuka was hit. Pieces of black metal started to fly from it. Desperately the German fought to keep control. The left wing broke off. It began to flutter to the ground like a great metal leaf.

'*We've got him... We've got the Fritz bastard!*' the gulag rats roared with delight and ceased firing to watch the end of the stricken German plane.

It was dramatic. Thick white glycol fumes pouring from its crippled engine, the pilot fighting to the very last to keep it on an even keel, it hit the ground on the west bank of the Don. Somehow the pilot righted it — for a couple of seconds. At 400 kilometres an hour, it ploughed through the thick snow, throwing up a huge white wake behind it. A tyre hit a rock. It burst with an explosion as if an 88mm had just blasted off. The Stuka lurched and shimmied. It swiped a fir. The fir snapped in half and the Stuka swung completely round, the pilot dead over his shattered controls. Next moment it disintegrated as its bombs exploded — one great, blinding white flash that had them blinking their eyes violently and then it was gone, festooning the trees all about with pieces of debris.

Glinka took his eyes off the lone wheel wobbling across the snow and said in an awed voice, 'God Almighty, what a way to go!' And then he remembered the other two planes and cried, 'All right, you slack-arsed shit-shovellers, let's get at it! *Davoi!*'

But the other two Stuka pilots had had enough. Abruptly they were off, winging their way eastwards once more, followed by a hail of angry but ineffectual fire from the gulag rats until Boldin cried, 'Cease firing … cease firing… Save your ammunition, men —' His words ended in a cry of alarm.

From the other side of the river, an ancient Skoda tank was slithering down from the German-held heights, followed by a cautious group of infantry in the khaki of the Romanian Army, each man bent as if advancing against a strong wind.

Obersturmbannführer Harsch was putting the second phase of his private war into action.

The Romanian lieutenant with the weak, affected, pale face and pencil-slim moustache, which looked to Harsch as if he painted it on every morning in front of his shaving mirror, had wandered into the little half-track laager, an hour after Harsch had extracted the promise from his cousin that the Stukas would cover his operation. The Romanian hadn't spoken any German, but with the help of Goldwasser's Italian, which had certain similarities with Romanian, and a lot of exaggerated gestures, they had discovered that the little Skoda tank was having engine trouble and was being taken to some Romanian workshops for repairs, escorted by a platoon of infantry as protection against partisans.

'That's *his* story, *Obersturmbannführer*,' Goldwasser said a little contemptuously, while the Romanian sipped Harsch's last bottle of champagne, his little finger with its manicured nail extended affectedly. 'My guess is that he's just bugged out from the front, knowing what was to come.'

'Exactly my own supposition,' Harsch said, smiling winningly at the young officer in his elegant tailored uniform and gleaming riding boots, complete, for some reason or other, with spurs. 'But that little Skoda could come in very handy, Goldwasser.'

'Perhaps, but I can't see our perfumed friend getting himself involved in anything even slightly dangerous.'

'Probably not,' Harsch agreed. 'But you know these Romanian cardboard soldiers do tend to lead from the rear. If I could assure him that he wouldn't have to do any fighting himself, but just keep his peasants moving in the general direction of the Popov's, we might pull it off.'

'What are you going to bribe him with? There is no more champers.'

'Have a good look at him, my clever little Jewish friend. What kind of chappie do you think he is?'

Goldwasser sniffed. 'Like *that*, is my guess.'

'My guess, too. A typical warm-brother … Goldwasser,' Harsch smiled again at the simpering Romanian, 'would you be so kind as to leave my HQ for a few moments? I should like to talk to our dear Romanian friend under — as it were — four eyes.'

Bewildered and a little hurt that he was being excluded from Harsch's confidence, Goldwasser had left and stood outside in the snow, watching the ragged Romanians in their tall fur hats, chattering away in their own tongue. He did not wait long.

Exactly five minutes later, Harsch came out of the tent with his arm round the shoulders of the Romanian officer to announce that the lieutenant was prepared to attack the bridge with his tank and infantry — naturally from a safe distance.

'But how?' Goldwasser asked when they were alone again. 'What was the bribe you used?'

'Me,' Harsch said simply. 'He's never had a German arse before. Obviously the idea excited him greatly. Apparently it will give him some degree of social status among his own kind in Bucharest. It's not every day that a Romanian homosexual gets a chance to fuck an Aryan beast, what!'

Goldwasser shook his head in mock wonder. The big SS colonel was as crazy as his men.

Now shouting threats and encouragement at his peasant infantry as they crept down the steep bank behind the roaring Skoda with its 37mm cannon switching from side to side suspiciously, and occasionally hurling rocks at those who shrank back, the Romanian lieutenant directed his 'attack' from behind a safe boulder, his mind full of things other than battle.

But the tank did the trick, however cowardly and undecided the infantry were. Its first shell went hopelessly wide, exploding harmlessly on the far bank, but its explosion was sufficient to panic the gulag rats at the western exit of the bridge. They started to pull back, firing as they withdrew, but pulling back all the same, deathly scared of those whirling tracks which could churn anyone unfortunate enough to fall beneath into a bloody pulp within seconds.

Boldin saw the danger at once. At the moment this was only a withdrawal, but the withdrawal could easily turn into a full-scale retreat. He had seen it happen before when infantry out in the open had been attacked by tanks.

'Vulf,' he cried to the little intellectual who was watching the scene with horrified interest, 'get the Fritz stovepipe. Quick!' For a moment it seemed as if Vulf had not understood. Then he remembered the meaning of the words; it was the Fritz soldiers' slang expression for the primitive Wehrmacht bazooka. He pelted into the little house where they had placed the weapons captured from the Germans guarding the bridge.

Panting, Vulf thrust the long, clumsy-looking antitank weapon into Boldin's hands, holding on to the rockets himself. 'What are —'

'Come on,' Boldin cut him short and started to run towards the bridge where the flak-cannon were firing all-out over the heads of the retreating soldiers, with the 20mm shells howling off the tank's sides in white blurs like ping-pong balls. 'Glinka,' he roared above the frenetic chatter of the cannon, 'try to drop your shells on to the infantry behind, and in the name of God, don't shoot us in the back!'

'Try not to comrade major,' Glinka said and raised his sights. 'It'd be the first time I've shot a major — one of ours, I mean.' He spat over the barrel.

Crouched low. the two officers ran forward, brushing the retreating infantry to both sides as they clattered on to the bridge, ignoring the bullets coming from the Skoda's turret as the gunner realized that these two men were not running away, but were intent on fighting.

Boldin grabbed a rocket and thrust it home. 'Fire at the turret-slit, Vulf,' he yelled above the rattle of machine-gun fire. 'Try to confuse the shit!'

He dropped to one knee, the rumbling Skoda a hundred metres away, a twentieth-century David facing up to an armoured Goliath. Hardly sighting the weapon flung across his right shoulder, knowing that if he didn't knock the Goliath out the very next second he'd be dead, Boldin fired.

A crack, a two-metre scarlet flame and the heavy black projectile was hurtling towards the Skoda, rotating crazily, trailing angry red sparks behind it. Crump! The Skoda reared up on its rear bogies and slammed down again with a tremendous thud that shook the very earth. One track slipped off like a severed limb. The tank, out of control, smashed into the side of the bridge and then slowly, very slowly, the gun barrel started to sink like the dying head of some primeval monster.

A minute later the ragged Romanian infantry were fleeing for their lives, throwing away their weapons in their crazed fear, simply brushing aside the young handsome officer as he tried to stop them streaming on to the steppe beyond and vanishing for good.

Five kilometres away, as the last half-track was successfully manoeuvred from the rough log raft, Harsch correctly interpreted the sudden end to the fire-fight beyond the forest. 'I have a strong feeling, my dear Goldwasser,' he said, watching the men clamber on board their half-tracks in preparation for the last stage of their drive, 'that our Romanian allies have received a bloody nose from the Popov's.'

'I expect you're right,' Goldwasser agreed as the fierce snap-and-crackle of rifle and machine-gun fire gave way to single shots and then died away altogether.

'Anyway,' Harsch said cheerfully, slapping his sword against the side of the half-track as a signal for the driver to start up and pleased at the success of his stratagem, 'now my pure Aryan arse is safe for a little while longer... Carbide!' he cried.

'Carbide,' the code-word for 'start' ran the length of the little column and the first half-track began to roll. The third phase of *Obersturmbannführer* Harsch's private war had commenced.

On the outskirts of Kalach, the little civilian relieved himself of his heavy rucksack and, taking out his binoculars with those fearsome hands of his, focused them with interest on the scene below.

The man from Smersh had arrived...

BOOK THREE: *THE MAN FROM SMERSH*

CHAPTER 1

The man from Smersh had been killing men — and women, too — since he was eight, a barefoot orphan from a godforsaken steppe village, one of the thousands of such children which the Civil War, the famine, and the warring armies, Czech, Russian, German, Japanese, French, American, Polish and all the rest, had swept into the cities.

It was not very surprising that he had begun murdering at that tender age. In that year of 1918, little girls sold themselves to men who could have been their grandfathers for a hunk of bread and a bowl of beans; boys who were belt-high to the soldiers did even worse things to keep themselves alive. But he could neither pander nor pimp. Instead he learnt to kill.

On the whole, it had been easy. He was a gentle, mild-mannered quiet boy, in spite of his ragged clothes and dirty face, who no one suspected when he came up to the Cheka HQ with his scraggy mongrel dog, which he left tied up outside while the feared policemen fed him with sweet cakes and spoonful's of honey. The bomb tied to the bell of the poor creature killed the lot of them half an hour after he had left.

It had been equally easy with the Red general who had given him a kiss on the forehead and invited the polite little boy into his private room. Whether for sexual reasons or just out of pity, the man from Smersh never found out, for the general did not live much longer after that invitation. He had plunged the razor-sharp dagger he had concealed in his ragged sleeve deep into the man's fat belly and ripped hard upwards. The general was dead even before he had slipped out of the window.

In the end the Cheka had caught him and the rest of the White terrorist band for which he had worked so successfully; it had been inevitable as the Communists had started to get the upper hand everywhere. But unlike the rest of the band who had soon been blown to eternity by heavy Mauser bullets in those notorious cellars in Kiev, he had survived. The Cheka chief had taken a fancy to him.

Of course, there had been the usual sexual unpleasantness which had put him off that form of relief and entertainment for good. Now what always excited his fantasy was violent death. The perverted Cheka chief had ensured that he had been trained and educated. It had therefore seemed natural that he would become one of the first ten recruits to the NKVD's newest department, Smersh. An angry Stalin had ordered Beria to set it up in the mid-thirties to take bloody revenge on the ever-increasing number of Communists who had become disillusioned with the Dictator and the Party.

They had been great days for him. He had murdered men — and women — all over Europe, travelling first class, dining in the best restaurants, staying in four-star hotels, seeing a world that he had not imagined could possibly exist. Then he had loved his job.

Once he had killed a traitor in Switzerland who had become a religious fanatic — often the case with those who had found the Communist god had failed them. He had dressed himself in a priest's soutane and broad-brimmed hat and met the traitor in a lonely walk where he had bent on his knees to receive a blessing. He'd received it all right: he had pulled the Mauser from the sleeve of his soutane and as the treacherous fool had knelt there humbly, he had blasted the back of his head off!

In Paris, he had shot an old pederast of a Secret Service general, who had defected, as he lay in a drugged sleep in the arms of some naked young French pavement artist.

Once he had even managed to get inside one of the new Fritz concentration camps and drown a renegade German Communist leader, who was suspected of betraying Comintern secrets to the fascists. He had plunged him inside the great forty-seater latrine. Beria had awarded him the Red Star for that job.

In early 1940 he had fallen from grace. He had been sent to Mexico to deal with the arch-traitor Trotsky once and for all, and put an end to his flood of anti-Stalin propaganda. But he had been detected attempting to break into his villa and only escaped by knifing one of the guards and thus raising the alarm. The job of driving the ice-pick into the Jew's skull had been left to the effete Belgian who now languished in a Mexican jail: a thought which still gave him some pleasure.

But the great days abroad were over. Now it was Soviet citizens who couldn't be silenced legally that he had to deal with. The Molotov Cocktail through the letterbox of the well-known Jewish surgeon suspected of being a Zionist; the hand-grenade fixed to the ignition of a Finnish Communist's car who was thought to be supplying information to the British Secret Service; the knife job on one of Beria's former mistresses who had threatened to 'reveal all' in a letter to *Novy Mir*; the hammer-blow on the head of the Latvian hunger-striker.

More than once he had thought he might ask for transfer to some other department of the NKVD, perhaps out to the camps, far away in Siberia where he might be able to rehabilitate himself in the eyes of Beria. But he found he could not exist without the thrill that killing gave him; the knowledge that in his hands lay the power of life or death over virtually everyone in the Soviet state. He reasoned that however unimportant or humble his new 'cases' (as he always called them) were, the fact that he was one of the handful of men in the USSR able to execute made him important, very important indeed. He stayed with Smersh.

Now on this chill November day, with the leaden clouds beginning to build rapidly, promising a snowstorm before the day was out, the man from Smersh considered how he was to tackle his present 'case'.

His professional pride and Beria's strict orders that the death of Colonel Katukov had to be publicly demonstrated to his soldiers so that they realized what the price of disobedience was made it impossible for him to kill the officer by means of a rifle with a telescopic sight. He would have to get so close to the 'case' that it would be inevitable that his soldiers would be involved. The question was: how would they react? They were a long way from Moscow here, and there were many of them. Would they calmly accept the fact that their colonel had been condemned to death in the capital and he had come from there to carry out the sentence?

Of course the man from Smersh knew that most of them were *tshestyni vor*, professional criminals, who owed allegiance only to themselves. But what of the rest, the kind of gulag rat he detested most: the anti-Communist, the ones who hated the Soviet system which had made him what he was? Would they tolerate the execution? He pondered the question in his little cave hiding-place. Finally, he decided that first he would make a reconnaissance. Veteran of half a hundred murders as he was and supremely confident in himself, he was no fool. First of all he had to find out how the land lay before he dealt with the 'case'. Slipping into his rucksack and shouldering his rifle, he set off for the orchard below as the first gentle flakes of snow began to drift down.

The man from Smersh was on his way for his own particular date with destiny: he was going to his last killing…

'Germany, *Germany without everything … without butter, without meat. Even our little bit of jam, the Admin eats!*' *Obersturmbannführer* Harsh sang softly to the tune of 'Deutschland Über Alles', swinging his broken sword to keep time as the half-tracks nosed their way through the ever-thickening snowfall towards the Russian-held bridge.

Now the snow was hitting the half-tracks' windscreens like a wall of white flak so that the drivers were forced to reduce speed in order to be able to see the road ahead. In this kind of weather, Goldwasser, crouched shivering next to the singing SS officer, told himself they could bump right into the Red positions without warning. As the snow fell in solid sheets, as if some God on high were determined to blot out this war-torn world for ever, Goldwasser wondered what Harsch would do. As if he could read the Italian officer's mind, Harsch leaned over, pressing his mouth close to Goldwasser's ear, for the wind had now reached hurricane force, and bellowed, 'Don't worry, my little Jewish friend. I'm not going to attack in this weather. Even the Führer's Fire Brigade is not that *meschugge*.'

Goldwasser smiled at the use of the Jewish word for 'crazy', and bellowed back, 'Then why don't we stop now, *Obersturm*?'

'Because this storm provides excellent cover. We can get right into the Popov positions without being discovered. The wind drowns the noise of the engines.'

'And then?'

'And then, my dear Goldwasser,' Harsch gave him an unholy smile, 'as befits two gents and officers, you and I will do a little recce.'

'Recce?' Goldwasser asked, feeling a cold finger of fear trace its way down his spine so that he had to shudder.

Harsch yelled, 'Yes, we'll recce their positions for the morning attack *personally*.'

Goldwasser groaned.

'I remember the crazy bastard once running through the whole camp naked,' Corporal Glinka recounted. 'He had a salt herring sticking out of his arse, shouting he was a mermaid! That was when the *telpluschka* arrived from Moscow with a fresh consignment of prisoners for the gulag. God, he must have put the wind up them! But he was like that. I remember the time that he promised he'd eat the commandant's pet dog if somebody would give him his tobacco ration.' He sighed at the memory. 'Those were the days, brothers. They'll never come back now.'

Vulf huddled next to Boldin, a blanket wrapped around his head, snorted '*Djavel!* That corporal must have had over his hundred of vodka Those were the days!' he sneered. 'Fun in the camp! Fun in the *telpluschka*!' He tapped his forehead. 'Absolutely, totally crazy!' Boldin nodded absently and wished the snowstorm would end so that he could get outside and check their front. The Stukas and the attack by the Romanians had obviously been the prelude to the main assault. But where was it? What had become of those SS and their half-tracks who had attacked them on the first day? Had they called off their attack because of the weather, or was there something else behind it? The thought worried him in spite of knowing that there were little groups of unfortunate gulag rats hidden in their ice-made positions out there in the raging storm. Not that he could see them in spite of the fact that it was still daylight; the storm was too intense.

'I remember the first time I saw the door of the *telpluschka* open to admit us prisoners,' Vulf was saying, 'I was nearly knocked over backwards by the stench. It hadn't been cleaned out from the last lot of prisoners so that the shit was knee-deep on the floor. They'd fed them rotten fish soup for three days and they'd died like flies from diarrhoea and choking on their own vomit, and now we were expected to undergo the same process. What a mess! Out of the seventy prisoners who set out with me, only twenty of us made it. Every day we shoved out ten or more dead when we halted at night for fish soup and more fish soup!'

'It's always been that way in Russia, little brother,' Boldin said, remembering how he had first gone to war in the large wooden goods wagon back in 1916 and how he had been transported to the camp in one after his disgrace twenty-odd years later, a marshal of the Soviet Union reduced to a 'faceless one', a mere number on the NKVD's arrest list. In the Czar's time then and Stalin's now. The *telpluschka* have always taken us Russians either to die in battle for the tyrant or to slave to death for him in some damned camp.'

Vulf nodded. 'I suppose you're right, Boldin.'

They fell silent again, listening to the howl of the wind and the patter of snowflakes on the little window of the *isba*.

'I think the Fritzes have got their arses in the bacon sheer,' Glinka said changing the subject. 'They got a bellyful this morning and they've buggered off. Besides, the Fritzes are easy put off by a couple of odd snowflakes.' He jerked a dirty thumb at the window, now almost packed with wet snow. 'They run for cover as soon as they see a bit o' white.'

Boldin smiled and wished he had Glinka's confidence. The Fritzes were out there somewhere, he could almost smell them, but where? — that was the question. And then he had his brainwave. 'Listen, you rats,' he announced, sitting up suddenly, 'you've been running off yer mouths too long, doing nothing while your comrades freeze their eggs off out there in the orchard.'

'Hard shit,' Glinka said. 'It'll be our turn tonight.'

'But till then, I've got a little job of work for your delicate lily-white paws.' Boldin said, taking a bullet out of his spare pistol magazine and then pulling out his combat knife. 'I'm going to show you how to make a deballocker that will really sit — so watch carefully because you're all going to be making them in five minutes' time. After all, we have to make our Fritz friends feel really warmly welcome if they chance to come stumbling through our positions this night.' Gritting his teeth, he scored his knife across the nose of the slug and then repeated the score in the other direction to form a cross. The deballocker was under construction.

CHAPTER 2

The clatter of the half-tracks was almost drowned by the howling wind. The infantry walking on both sides of them as they advanced through the whirling snow were bent like old men, their uniforms whipped tight against their skinny bodies, the snowflakes clinging to their faces so that every few moments they had to wipe their eyes clear in order to see where they were going.

Now it was nearly dawn, the time, Harsch knew, when the Popov outposts were most likely to be dozing, especially in a storm like this. After all, who in his right mind would attack in weather like this? Only the Führer's Fire Brigade, he told himself wryly.

His plan was simple. It had to be under such conditions. The half-tracks would stick to what was still left of the road, while his grenadiers came in on both flanks, working their way through the Popov positions which he and Goldwasser had reconnoitred two hours before. When he judged they were in position, his red flare would be the signal for a bold, quick attack — for which the Führer's Fire Brigade was famous. With luck he would roll up the Popov's, in spite of their superior numbers, before they knew what had hit them.

The forest on both sides of the road had begun to thin. The wind howled straight across the steppe and, unprotected by the firs now, it made their progress even more difficult. The countryside was dead, as if it had been abandoned long ago to this cruel snow. They filed by a dead cow, already half buried by the snow, its legs sticking rigidly upwards so that it looked like a tethered barrage balloon.

Harsch narrowed his eyes to slits and peered through the whirling flakes. With difficulty, he could just make out the smudge of the new trees, the orchard, in which lay the main Popov positions on this side of the bridge. He tapped the driver on the shoulder and he slowed down even more. 'Bail out!' he commanded.

Like the veterans they were, the grenadiers rolled over the sides of the still-moving half-track, bodies held low so that they didn't present too big a target, and dropped into the snow. Harsch, gripping his sword, followed equally expertly for a man with one hand; and more awkwardly, Goldwasser.

A minute later the line of half-tracks, now occupied only by the driver and the gunner manning the 20mm cannon, disappeared into the snowstorm. Harsch waited till the last one's tail convoy light had vanished, then commanded, *'Mir nach!'*

Unslinging their weapons, ready for action, the grenadiers started to file after the big colonel up in the lead, with Igor slightly to his front and Goldwasser at his side.

The minutes passed. There was no sound save their own harsh breathing and the howl of the wind. In front Igor stumbled on, his head bent, sniffing the air like a tracker dog. 'He can *smell* Popov's, that one,' Harsch explained to Goldwasser, 'In this shitty weather, I'm glad of him. He won't let us stumble into some Popov shit heap.'

Goldwasser mumbled something, and Harsch said, 'If I survive this war, I'm going to take Igor back to the Reich with me. With him I won't need to keep any expensive hunt —'

His words were interrupted by a slight, dry crack like the breaking of a brittle twig in high summer. In the brief flash of blue light, Goldwasser caught a glimpse of Igor, screaming until his screams were drowned by the snow, clutching at his crotch and falling.

Harsch sprang forward. He turned his servant over. Igor lay there gasping like a stranded fish. Hastily Harsch thrust the blade of his sword into Igor's mouth to prevent his tongue curling backwards and choking him.

'Here,' Harsch commanded while all around him the grenadiers crouched, their weapons at the ready, eyes peering through the snow to their front, 'take the flash. Let's see what happened.'

Goldwasser pulled the little torch off the lapel of Harsch's tunic and clicked the switch.

In the circle of faint blue light, he could see from Igor's face that the little Ukrainian was dying. His eyelids were flickering rapidly and his nose was already beginning to take on that cream-white, pinched look of the dying.

'Run it over his body,' Harsch ordered. 'Let's see what hit him.'

Carefully, Goldwasser did so and then he gasped with shocked revulsion. 'In God's name!' he began and couldn't continue.

'A deballocker,' Harsch said bitterly. 'Since our little recce, the Ivan bastards have slipped out and sown a deballocker minefield.'

'But what is a ... deballocker.'

'Something only those Popov pigs could think up,' Harsch snarled, stroking the dying man's forehead, as his body heaved now with the final agony of death. 'A dum-dum bullet attached to the cartridge and a spring. Step on it and you're circumcised more thoroughly than any of your rabbis could do it.'

At his side, Igor's head fell to one side. Gently, very gently, Harsch drew his sword out of the dead man's mouth. 'He wasn't a bad bastard,' he said and closed his servant's eyes for good.

'What now?' Goldwasser asked, shuddering at the thought of the terrible death which lay just in front of them.

'Don't worry, Goldwasser, I won't let you have your thing docked any shorter. Now it's going to be up to the half-tracks. We'll make our way back to the road and follow them up.'

He rose to his feet and pulled out his Very pistol. Raising it, he cried the battle-cry of the armed SS — '*Alles für Deutschland* —' and pressed the trigger.

The signal flare hissed into the howling sky and burst into a bright, unreal light, bathing all below in its blood-red colour. The battle for the orchard had commenced.

'Fritzes … the Fritzes are coming …'

The cries of alarm and fear pierced the howling storm as the half-tracks, racing at full speed, their cannon chattering, appeared out of the storm, heading straight for the forward posts.

What happened next was a massacre. The half-tracks simply rolled over the gulag rat positions, the drivers swinging their heavy vehicles round and round on the slick ice, catching glimpses of white, terrified faces below them, as they churned the occupants to bloody pulp, moving on to the next position, tracks red with blood. Here and there the rats had somehow managed to bury into the iron-hard earth and thought themselves proof even against the ten-ton half-tracks. They had not reckoned with Harsch's veterans. Blocking the whole top of the hole, they gunned their engines. Thick grey, choking smoke filled the pits. Clutching their throats, coughing horribly, the rats suffocated and the half-tracks clattered on to commence their deadly work once again.

Boldin, pistol in hand, firing at the white blaze of the attacking vehicles' flak-cannon, knew the position was lost. Already individual gulag rats were rising panic-stricken from their holes and positions, tossing away their weapons and beginning to run for the rear. It would be only a matter of moments before the whole position crumpled irretrievably. He had to rescue what could still be rescued. 'Vulf,' he called above the screams of the dying and the terribly mutilated men in the front positions. 'Try to blind the drivers with your Very pistol... I must get the rest of them out... Back off to Colonel Katukov's positions around the HQ!'

'*Horoscho!*' Vulf understood immediately. Crouching there, he fired his first red Very light directly at the nearest half-track. It burst on the vehicle's ugly metal snout. Red, blinding light shot up. The driver braked instinctively, thinking he had been hit by a bazooka-rocket and when he realized he hadn't, swung his vehicle round to escape into the white gloom.

Boldin dashed forward, kicking and slamming his pistol butt at the terrified gulag rats, snarling commands, snapping off wild, hopeless shots at the half-tracks whirling in and out of the stunted, snow-heavy apple trees like primeval monsters hunting their quarry. '*Back ... back ... in the name of hell, withdraw to the colonels HQ!*' he yelled, blinded every time that Vulf spotted one of the marauding German vehicles and fired, bathing the trees in that glowing, unreal blood-red light.

Somehow or other he brought some order into the unholy mess. Firing as they went, the gulag rats started to back off. Boldin was everywhere, missing death by seconds time and time again, herding his men to the big, squat HQ, while the half-tracks pushed home their advantage.

And then suddenly, as was the case with all attacks, the steam went out of it. The firing and the pressure died away. Now could be heard the screams of the abandoned wounded as they died among the shattered trees of the orchard, as Harsch's infantry rejoined the half-tracks to protect them from some bold bazooka man who had elected to remain behind and deal with the vulnerable armoured vehicles.

Sweating heavily in spite of the biting cold as he fought the survivors back to the centre of the battalion's defences, Boldin knew well that heart-breaking wail: an explosive bullet to the lung or something of that kind. The gut shot and the thigh shot died easily; the blood had run out of them before they knew what had happened to their poor, mutilated bodies. But the lung shot and the head shot, they died slowly and horribly.

The little hairs erect at the back of his head, Boldin herded the rats through those scythed-off trees, ears full of those terrible cries, forcing himself by an effort of sheer will-power not to abandon the retreat and go rushing backwards to finish them off with a shot.

Then they were flooding Katukov's positions and Vulf was helping him through the door into the warmth streaming out from the great green-tiled oven which dominated the colonel's room. And Katukov was saying, 'Now we are really in the shit, Boldin! Really deep in it up to our hooters!' as if he, Boldin, were responsible for the defeat in the orchard.

'So, this is our position,' Katukov said, his nerve recovered after the shock of that rout in the orchard, ignoring the thud-thud of the German flak-cannon against the thick walls of his HQ. 'We hold this place and a line,' with a borrowed bayonet he traced a line on the dust of the floor, 'up to the bridge, with both exits from it in our hands.'

Another burst of 20mm shells stitched a furious pattern on the wall outside and Vulf commented cynically, 'For a little while longer at least.'

Katukov ignored him. 'My estimate of their strength is that they are reinforced company size. We outnumber them considerably.'

'Yes, comrade colonel, but they've got armour of a sort and mobile cannon. All we've got is rifle and machine-gun power — and if I may be so bold to say so, we're bogged down in this place, whereas they've got mobility on their side!' Boldin said.

At the far end of the room, Glinka, pouring shredded tobacco on an open wound in his right arm by way of antiseptic, was saying contemptuously, 'When it comes to being shit-arsed smart, those rats up front are like the feller who carries a fork with him all the time in case it rains pea soup. They should have been expecting something like that after we'd spent half the shitting night spreading deballockers on both sides of the road. But no, they lay in their ice-palaces sawing wood, while the Fritzes sneaked up on them and gave them the real old purple shaft — right up the arse!'

Boldin smiled a little wearily. Glinka's assessment of the situation wasn't exactly staff college, but it served well enough. They had been caught napping. Now the question was: what should they do?

Katukov seemed to be able to read the big major's mind for he said, 'I propose a counter-attack to restore our positions in the orchard. We must keep the Fritzes as far away from the bridge as possible. That is essential.'

'With what?' Vulf asked.

Again Katukov ignored the question, but Boldin didn't. 'Colonel,' he said sombrely, 'a counter-attack against those mobile flak-cannon would be sheer suicide. They'd slaughter us. The attack would come to a standstill within five minutes. Quite purposeless,' he ended, without emotion. 'We don't stand a chance.'

'And what do you suggest, *marshal*?' Katukov emphasized the old rank with a sneer.

'Marshal or major,' Boldin controlled his anger, 'I'm giving you a simple soldier's thoughts on the subject.'

'They are?'

'Twofold. Either we try some sort of surprise flank attack and catch them off guard, or —' he hesitated.

'Get on with it, man!'

'We abandon the position tonight as soon as it's dark. They haven't the infantry to stop —'

'Abandon the position!' Katukov cut in brutally. 'What are you saying, Boldin?'

'I think I made my meaning quite clear, comrade colonel,' Boldin said coldly. 'I have backed you up so far because I thought you might be right and have a chance of succeeding. Now I don't think you have. Sooner or later the Fritzes will bring their full weight to bear upon us and our effort will have been for nothing. All that will result from it is that another eight hundred *matkas* somewhere back there to the east will weep for dead sons — to no purpose.' He shrugged expansively. 'All to no avail.'

'But in thirty-six hours the great offensive will start,' Katukov protested. 'It is vital to its success that we hold the bridge 'till then.'

'*If* it starts,' Vulf said.

'My concern is my gulag rats,' Boldin added his final words to the discussion.

Katukov stared glumly at the ground.

At the far end of the room Glinka was saying, as if to emphasize the problem, for their food was beginning to run out too, 'Brothers, I'd sell my arse for a piece of good sausage now — even *bad* sausage. I'm that goddamned hungry!' Nobody laughed. It was a sign of the mood they were in.

Katukov raised his head. 'Boldin, give me one more chance.' He looked at Boldin, eyes pleading. 'Let me have that last counter-attack. If it fails, *you* decide.' Boldin looked at the big colonel, his face tortured with emotion.

'All right,' he made his decision. 'One last time. After that, Katukov, I give the orders…'

CHAPTER 3

'What will the Fritzes do, little brother?' Boldin asked, trying to out-think the Germans somewhere out there in the howling storm.

'Am I Jesus?'

'If Jesus were a little four-eyed homosexual, yes!' Boldin said with a short laugh.

Vulf didn't share it.

'My guess is that they will attempt to cut us off from the bridge,' Boldin went on. 'After all, that is the important thing — the bridge.'

'So?' Vulf asked, a little annoyed by the reference to his sexual habits and this tactical rambling which didn't interest him one bit.

'When will the Fritzes make an attempt, where will they be at the time and how can we turn the situation to our advantage? Three small questions with —'

'Large answers,' Vulf beat him to it.

'Exactly.'

'As far as they are concerned,' Boldin said, thinking aloud, 'we're as good as prisoners tied up in this place. They can contain us with a handful of infantry and make the dash for the bridge with their half-tracks.'

'Oh, Boldin,' Vulf groaned, 'what does that damned bridge really matter? Do you think anyone will give a damn about it in a couple of days' time? It might rate a couple of lines in *Pravda* in due course, but that'll be about it. Somebody might read them — after they've read the details of the latest ration issue, of course.'

Boldin laughed shortly. 'I suppose you're right, Vulf, you little cynic. Why do wretches like us, the scum of the camps fight and die for that piece of architecture out there? There'll be no glory in it for us. You can be sure your *Pravda* won't mention that it was captured and held by the gulag rats. That honour will go to some Guards regiment or other.' He shrugged. 'But I suppose it's in the blood — of an old soldier like myself, I mean. We fight for the sake of fighting.'

Again Vulf grunted and lapsed into silence, leaving Boldin to his deliberations.

At the other end of the room, Katukov was thinking hard, too. He had come to the same conclusion as Boldin that as soon as visibility improved, the Fritzes would rush the bridge with their half-tracks; it would be a typical bold German tactic. But in doing so, as always with the *Blitzkrieg* methods the Fritzes favoured, they would offer their flank, yet what could the gulag rats do with that open flank? The only heavy weapons were on the bridge and they had used the last of the rockets for the captured 'stove-pipe'. How could infantry armed only with rifles and machine-guns stop armour? And then he remembered the old days of the revolution and he had it. He stood up abruptly. 'Boldin,' he called, startling the men slumped dozing on the straw-covered floor, 'Molotov Cocktails!'

Boldin clicked his fingers excitedly, then his smile vanished as quickly as it had appeared. 'But where do we get the gas from, colonel?'

Katukov had his answer ready. 'The Skoda. It must have at least half a tank full of gas.'

Boldin snapped into action at once. 'Glinka, you rogue!'

Glinka woke up reluctantly from an exciting dream in which he had been sitting at a table groaning under the weight of succulent hams and tender roast chicken. 'Yes, comrade major?'

'Glinka, you are the greatest rogue in the battalion. If anyone can get something — before it gets lost, it is Corporal Glinka.'

Glinka looked down at his hands. 'Things just seem to stick to them, comrade,' he said. 'Can't explain how it always happens to poor old Glinka.' He sighed, as if the cares of the world weighed heavy on his shoulders.

'All right, *poor, old* Glinka,' Boldin said, amused by the broad-backed rogue, 'I'm going to give you the chance of doing some official looting.'

Glinka's eyes narrowed, while Katukov frowned, displeased at the manner in which Boldin was handling this business. One didn't joke about such important military matters. 'What do you mean exactly, comrade?' he asked suspiciously.

'Glinka, you know that Romanian tin can out there?' Glinka nodded.

'My information is that it contained some very nasty Romanian sausage. Someone reported that he could smell bacon in it, too. It's all yours — if you can bring back all the gas the tank contains.'

'So that's it, eh, comrade? I thought it was too good to be true. You want me to stick my bacon in the slicer to bring back the gas, eh?'

Boldin laughed. 'Glinka, I could order you, but I'm not. I'm dangling a bit of bait in front of your greedy optics to make you — er-volunteer.'

Glinka considered a moment or two. He knew from past experience that tank crews turned their vehicles into mobile stores. The ordinary stubble-hopper had to hump all his stuff; as a result he didn't carry much. Not the tanker. Anything he could lay his oily paws on was pushed aboard; after all he didn't have to carry it. He licked his lips greedily. Those Romanians were reputedly great chow-hounds. 'All right, comrade major, I am ready to volunteer for this hazardous mission with my section.'

'What!' came the cries of alarm from his men lying in the straw, 'We didn't volunteer, corporal!'

'Of course, yer did,' Glinka said easily, reaching for his machine-pistol. 'Yer were just too shy, that's all. Now move those lazy arses of yours! Find what buckets and cans you can — come on, get the lead out!' He turned back to Boldin, grinning from ear to ear. 'Do you think Old Leather Face'll award me the Order of Red Salami for this one, comrade major?'

Katukov glared at him.

Five minutes later, Corporal Glinka was gone into the raging snow storm. Boldin would never see him again...

Back in the house, the others settled down to wait.

The little patrol battled through the snowstorm, chewing the extra ration of biscuit that Boldin had allowed them, encouraged at regular intervals by Glinka's 'There'll be Romanian brandy for all the canned goulash!' as they fought against the wind, heading in the general direction of the bridge.

They blundered into their own positions around the twin flak-cannon at this side of the bridge and nearly got shot by a trigger-happy sentry, who was startled by their sudden appearance out of the swirling white flakes. They were saved by Glinka's quick: 'Shoot me, yer son-of-a-whore and I'll jam yer rifle so far up yer arse that yer tonsils pop!'

There they halted for a few minutes to get their breath back and warm their frozen limbs by the fire which the gunners had got burning in the gun-pit. Then they set off again, now in battle formation as they passed their last post on the other side of the bridge, straining their eyes for the first glimpse of the wrecked Skoda.

Glinka stumbled over the snow-shrouded body of a dead Romanian soldier and called, 'Over here, brothers! Come on. Follow me!'

A couple of minutes later they blundered right into the little tank and while Glinka pushed aside the dead gunner and began to search eagerly for food and drink, his patrol filled their cans and bucket with the precious petrol they would need to make the Molotov Cocktails.

But Glinka was in for a disappointment. All he could find in the confused mess of the wrecked tank was a dried-up piece of sausage, heavily spiced with garlic to disguise the cheap horsemeat that it was made from. Miserably he swallowed it, telling himself that there had to be some food somewhere. His stomach was doing back-flips with hunger, rumbling menacingly like an angry lion, and when Corporal Glinka's stomach did back-flips, there was trouble brewing, unless the 'inner pig-dog', as he often called it to himself, was satisfied.

He sniffed the air, finishing the rest of the horsemeat sausage hurriedly before the others discovered him eating, listening to their hushed chatter as they emptied the Skoda's tank. Suddenly his eyes lit up. There was no mistaking it., Somewhere out there in the flying white gloom there was hot, frying pork-belly. His trained nose twitched. There was no doubt at all. *Frying pork-belly made of real pig!*

He rose hastily and wiped the back of his hairy hand across his wet lips so that the rest of the patrol would not be able to see the 'food-wake', as he called it, and clambered out into the storm. 'Listen, you barn-shitters, make tracks and get back to the HQ,' he ordered.

They looked up at him, their faces wet with snowflakes. 'Where's the chow?' one of them asked.

'Don't you worry about that, arse with ears!' Glinka rapped, excited beyond measure by that wonderful smell of frying pork. 'Leave the worrying to Corporal Glinka. That's what he's paid for.'

'But you promised!' someone objected.

'Do you want a knuckle sandwich?' Glinka said threateningly, doubling his fist into a small steam-shovel. 'Start counting yer ivories if you do.'

'But you said —'

'Listen,' he drowned the protest, 'if I find anything you'll get your share. Now off you go. I'll follow yer up. Move it!'

Reluctantly they started to trail away, bearing their heavy burdens until the storm swallowed them up. Glinka chuckled, telling himself that some idiot of a Romanian peasant had got himself a lump of meat out there and was indulging in a little bit of private chowtime. It would be as easy as falling off a log. He slung his tommy gun and pulled the long knife out of his felt boot. Crouching low, sniffing the snow-filled air at regular intervals, he started to trail that delicious odour.

The man from Smersh crouched in the low cave, considering his situation while he ate. He had just consumed one of the special cans of soup which Churchill had sent from England for the use of Russia's partisans. When you pulled a cartridge in the middle, the can heated of its own accord. Now he was roasting a large piece of salt pork on a spit above the solid-fuel cooker which could fold up into his pocket — again a gift from that whisky-swilling plutocrat in London.

He had been witness to the Fritz half-track attack which had stopped him in his attempt to break into the gulag rat position and carry out Beria's orders. Now he wondered what he should do next. He had no wish to clash with the Germans. He did not fear them. But he was realist enough to know that he had not the power over them that he had over his fellow countrymen. Everywhere in Soviet Russia, the very name 'Smersh' had a paralysing effect on his fellow countrymen. In Russia, he could walk into any community and dominate it. But not with the Fritzes. He cooked his meat, listening to the sizzle and splash of the fat as it dropped on the cooker, and discussed with himself in the fashion of lonely men, what he should do. It was thus that Corporal Glinka discovered him.

'Russian?' he asked, standing there at the entrance of the cave, knife in hand, greedy little eyes fixed on the cooking meat.

The man from Smersh jumped with surprise and then, trying to check his jingling nerves as he saw the uniform, answered, 'Yes … yes, I am Russian.'

Glinka lowered his knife. 'Nice bit of pig-meat you got there, comrade,' he said, his mind too full of food to ask what a civilian was doing out here, cooking a prime piece of pork.

'Do you want some?' the man from Smersh asked, recovering quickly.

'Can a duck swim?' Glinka said eagerly, the saliva trickling down his bearded chin now. Whatever doubts he may have had were overcome by the delicious scent of food and the strange civilian's polite, mild manner; the man couldn't be dangerous.

The man from Smersh handed him the spit and said, 'Help yourself.'

Glinka reached over eagerly and with his knife sawed off a chunk of the meat. 'Better than getting yer leg over a fat-titted whore,' he gurgled and bit deep into the meat, letting the grease run down his chin.

'I wouldn't know,' replied the man from Smersh, taking in the tattoos on Glinka's fingers and the blue marks on the back of his neck with the legend 'Chop Here'. The man was obviously a professional criminal. All the signs were there. 'What is the situation over there?' he asked.

'Shitty, decidedly shitty,' Glinka answered, mouth full of pork.

'What do you mean?' the man from Smersh asked, telling himself that the firing he had heard early on had been that of the Germans or Romanians after all. He had been right not to go into the gulag rats' camp.

'We expect the Fritzes to attack with armour as soon as this snow stops. That's why we were just near here. We were getting gas for Molotov Cocktails.'

'Your colonel intends to defend the place then?' the little civilian asked.

'Yes, he's a hard-arsed bastard, that Katukov. Typical Greenhat,' Glinka answered, gnawing at the meat. 'Hey, how did you know —' Glinka's startled query ended as the thin wire cut deep into his throat. He died with his mouth full of uneaten pork. Presumably it would have been the way that Corporal Glinka, the comedian of the 333rd Punishment Battalion, would have wanted to die.

CHAPTER 4

Silence!

The thump-thump of the flak cannon against the walls of the HQ had stopped at last.

Men looked at each other significantly. From above, in the look-out tower the sentry cried, 'The snow's letting up, comrade colonel.'

Katukov stared at Boldin. 'This is it, then?'

Boldin nodded grimly. 'Yes,' he said, 'we'd better get off.'

He turned to the gulag rats, armed with the crude petrol bombs, who were to be covered by the rest. 'Don't take any stupid risks,' he warned. 'Throw the things and then go to ground straightaway. Clear?'

'Clear,' they answered, knowing that they were potential suicide candidates.

Now from the direction of the orchard where the Germans were came the rumble of engines starting with difficulty in the cold dawn air.

Up in the watchtower the sentry cried excitedly, 'I think I can see them, comrades.'

Katukov, who would hold the house in case the Germans did make an attack on it, swept a quick look round the men posted at the windows and nodded his satisfaction and then, surprisingly for that unemotional man, stuck out his hand to Boldin. 'Good luck, brother,' he said.

Shocked into silence by the gesture, Boldin took it and then his group was out the door. Little Vulf, who was to remain behind, was shaking his head and telling himself not many of them would survive the next hour. He attempted to fix the look on Boldin's bold, broad face in his mind's eye in case he never saw him again; and then Boldin, too, was gone into the last flakes of snow.

The ten half-tracks burst out of the orchard at widely separated points and then, as prearranged, formed up into a large open arrowhead with Harsch's own vehicle in the centre and directly beyond the point so that he could control the attack by hand signals if necessary. Satisfied that they were all in their positions, Harsch pumped his one arm up and down rapidly three times, the infantry signal for 'at the double' and then they were off, a steel wedge of racing, roaring vehicles heading straight for the bridge. Almost immediately the two flak guns some 500 metres away opened up. White tracer shells started to curve through the grey air towards them, gathering speed every instant.

Goldwasser flashed a look at Harsch, holding on the best he could as the half-track rattled and swayed over the rough ground. There was no fear on the German's cruelly handsome face, just excitement, boundless excitement.

Wham! ... *wham!* ... *wham!*.... Goldwasser ducked instinctively, as a salvo of shells pumped a line of gleaming holes the length of the half-track. But still it raced on through that hail of fire.

Now the air was full of searing purple flame, the acrid, choking stink of burnt cordite, whirling copper shell-bands and fist-sized pieces of flying metal. A half-track was hit in the engine. It rolled to a stop, smoke pouring from the shattered motor. Immediately the grenadiers flung themselves over the sides and dropped to the snow, their weapons chattering.

The wild drive continued. They burst through the thin line of defenders who scattered immediately, throwing away their weapons in panic. Next instant they went down screaming under the flailing tracks of the armour, bodies pressed flat like cardboard in the snow.

Now the lead half-tracks were firing flat out themselves, their fire concentrated on the two flak guns holding the bridge only four hundred metres away. Fountains of snow and earth spouted up in great rolling clouds all around them and a terrified, yet mesmerized Goldwasser could see the tracer slugs howling white and red from the steel girders of the bridge. Still the flak guns kept firing, though their gunners were badly rattled now and their fire was scattered.

'*Heaven, arse and cloudburst!*' Harsch cried exuberantly, waving his broken sword. 'This is the life, Goldwasser, eh?' He grinned down at the white-faced Italian. 'Don't worry, my friend, you can only die once — and think — you can give your life for Adolf Hitler! What a —'

His words were drowned by the rending crash of one of the half-tracks, its windscreen a spider's web of smashed glass, its headless driver sprawled over the shattered wheel, slamming into one of the little *isbas*, completely out of control, scattering dead and dying men in its wake.

Harsch frowned and in a more subdued voice said, 'Two gone, eight to go.'

They raced on. Now the bridge was only 300 metres away.

'Here they come.' Boldin hissed, wiping the sweat off his hand and taking up his bottle again.

All around him in the ditch, his men did the same. Behind them, the second line, armed with rifles and tommy guns, prepared to cover them.

Boldin narrowed his eyes. The half-tracks were rattling across the rough, snow-heavy ground at an amazing speed. In a minute they would be almost parallel with them, at perhaps fifty metres' distance. The trick would be to rush them, fling their homemade bombs and duck; and Boldin had no illusions about how many would survive that wild rush.

He began to count out loud. '*One … two … three … four.*' His men tensed. '*Five … six…*' They lit the rough wicks that led into the deadly mixture. '*Seven … eight … nine!*' The half-tracks were almost upon them now. '*Ten… FORWARD A-T-T-A-C-K!*'

And then they were up, crouched low, racing for the nearest half-tracks, screaming loudly while behind them their comrades sent a stream of covering fire over their heads. The Germans spotted them almost at once. The grenadiers raised themselves up above the protective steel sides, knowing instinctively what the men running towards them across the snow were attempting to do.

A soldier next to Boldin screamed and stumbled into him. He pushed the wounded rat to one side. Fortunately. Next instant the bottle he was carrying burst into flames, streaming its fiery contents all over the unfortunate man, turning him immediately into a human torch.

Harsch saw the danger at once. He dropped his sword and placed his hand, fingers outspread, on the top of his helmet, the infantry signal for 'rally on me', crying furiously, 'Back off. Great crap on the Christmas tree — *Back off!*'

Too late!

Already the first bomber had got within throwing range, staggering through the falling bodies of his comrades who were going down on all sides, braving the wall of fire being put up by the desperate grenadiers. Screaming obscenities, he lobbed his bomb at the half-track in the very same instant that a burst of schmeisser fire ripped open his chest and sent him staggering backwards.

The bomb burst with a soft plop against the side of the half-track, splashing gasoline everywhere which ignited immediately. In a flash, the grenadiers were ablaze, the deadly, searing flame burning the length of the vehicle like a gigantic blow-torch.

Boldin in the lead, fighting his way through his dying men, screaming with agony as they fell, clapping bloody hands to ruined faces, chests, limbs, reeled back at that tremendous heat, his nostrils assailed by the sickening stench of burning flesh, as the terrible flames shrivelled the trapped, screaming grenadiers into charred pygmies, as the half-track careered on, trailing flames behind it.

Out of the smoke and flame came another. He didn't hesitate. Ignoring the slugs cutting up little spurts of snow all around his running feet, he pelted within twenty metres of the half-track so that he could see the pale-faced young Germans with their silver SS runes and death's-head badges and flung his Molotov Cocktail. Next instant he flung himself headlong into the snow, the burst intended for his chest missing him by millimetres.

The bomb exploded against the half-track. The driver bailed out, leaving the screaming grenadiers to their fate. A couple of them fell over the side and began running in panic, their bodies wreathed in the cruel, voracious flames until finally they fell and the flames consumed their agony-racked bodies.

Now the half-tracks started to veer off to the left away from the bomb-throwers, and Harsch told himself he knew the signs; the steam was going out of his attack. In a minute some fool of a driver would throw in reverse, slam into the half-track behind and the panic would start. Even in the elite Fire Brigade, such things could happen. Fire terrorized even the best-trained veteran. He had to do something before the rot set in.

'Driver … move it!' he bellowed above the confused racket all around. He flashed a look at the man. it was Adolfo, 'the Führer's Spanish Bastard', as the swarthy volunteer was called in the Brigade. '*Vamos andando!*' he yelled, pointing his broken sword to the left flank of what was left of his flying arrowhead.

'*Si*, si!' Adolfo yelled back and swung his wheel half left with a snarled '*Hijos de puta!*' at the bomb-throwers.

'What are you going to do, *Obersturmbannführer*?' Goldwasser cried, holding on for grim death as the halftrack heeled wildly.

'Take over the point myself! They'll follow me. I'll get them away from those damned Popov bombers. Come on, Adolfo, *carbide!*'

A bomber loomed up out of the fog of war. Harsch's gunner pressed his trigger. The man's stomach was ripped apart. He stumbled away, dragging his guts across the snow behind him. Another bomber came into view. Again the machine-gun chattered frenetically. A sudden line of holes etched themselves across the Russian's chest. The bomb fell from his nerveless fingers and exploded on the ground. The half-track clattered through it and Goldwasser's nose was suddenly full of the stink of singed hair — his own.

Now the other half-tracks started to swing towards Harsch's as he urged his driver to take the lead. Weaving in and out of the slower ones, Adolfo swung the ten ton vehicle from side to side, as if it weighed ten hundredweight, brilliantly avoiding a collision at the very last minute. Now the bridge was only 200 metres away, and in front of them there were only the two flak cannon and a handful of Russian infantry. It looked as if *Obersturmbannführer* Harsch was going to capture the bridge at Kalach at last.

CHAPTER 5

Steel flew everywhere.

A yellow-white spurt of flame at 100 metres' range and the half-track just behind Harsch's disintegrated. In a series of glowing red lumps of metal, what was left hurtled across the bridge road. The body of a grenadier slammed against the side of Harsch's half-track and burst like an over-ripe melon. Goldwasser screamed with absolute fear as hot blood drenched him.

The tracks clattered on to the hard-packed snow. The flak cannon was only fifty metres away now. Harsch could see the crew, their faces contorted with fear, flinging shell after shell into the rack in order to stop this metal monster that was heading straight for them on a collision course. A stream of 20mm shells scythed the half-track. Behind Goldwasser, a grenadier went down, arms flailing. Goldwasser began to blubber like a little child.

Twenty-five metres! Harsch saw the loader throw down the shells and start to pelt for the other side of the bridge. The half-track rocked crazily. The left track shot off. '*Como!*' Adolfo screamed and fought the half-track which was swaying from side to side like a drunkard.

Ten metres! The gunners scattered wildly. Like a steel mountain, the half-track, filled with dead and dying men, towered above the flak cannon. The stink of explosive and hot oil filled the air. There was a great rending crash. The half-track came to an abrupt halt. Adolfo smashed against the windscreen, teeth flying out of a suddenly blood-filled mouth. Slowly, terribly slowly, the gun and the half-track began to tilt, a mixture of wrecked, tangled metal and chunks of mangled bodies.

A lone gulag rat, crazed beyond measure, attempted to rush the stalled half-track. He slipped on the shredded flesh and blood and fell. Spitting out his teeth, Adolfo let him have a burst with his m.p., lisping, '*Maldita sea la madre!*'

The gulag rat rolled over and lay still.

A second half-track made the bridge — and a third.

At the second flak gun the crew fired one last tremendous burst. The half-track driver flung up his hands in agony. Completely out of control the half-track shot clean into the air and plunged into the Don. An obscene belch of trapped air and it had gone for good. And then the Russian gunners were fleeing for their lives. Colonel Harsch's men, what was left of them, had pulled it off at last. The bridge at Kalach was in German hands once again.

The man from Smersh was not very expert on matters of war, but he recognized that even with the handful of men at Harsch's disposal and the three battle-scarred half-tracks now blocking both ends of the bridge, the one-armed Fritz making his dispositions down below was in a good position. His men were protected by their armour, however small their number; it would be a tough nut for the gulag rat renegades to crack without heavy weapons. That is, he told himself, if they didn't simply fade away now that the Fritzes had got through.

He squatted at the entrance of his little cave, surveying the bustling Fritzes through his binoculars, wondering what he should do. Now he was cut off by the Fritzes from the man he had come to kill. Should he simply turn about and make his way back to the Russian positions in Stalingrad, leaving his mission uncompleted? Almost instantly he rejected that solution. He had had one failure; Beria wouldn't tolerate another. And he had no illusions about what would happen to a Smersh man who incurred Beria's displeasure. The Smersh killers knew too much. It would be a bullet at the back of his skull.

He considered the matter thoroughly while the big Fritz officer moved back and forth across the bridge, followed by a smaller officer in a uniform which he couldn't recognize, preparing for the counter-attack that he obviously expected the gulag rats to launch.

He and his men were SS, he knew that. He knew, too, that they fought to the very end. They had no alternative. Invariably the Russian infantry slaughtered them if they fell into their hands. But how steadfast, he asked himself, were they when they were leaderless? Would they stand and fight if he killed their officer?

The man from Smersh squatted there and thought out the problem.

Harsch was flushed with victory though he knew now from his own count that he had taken heavy losses. In all, he had only sixty men, including the wounded, to hold the bridge. Still, he was confident that with the protection of the half-tracks and the firepower they provided, he could do so until relief arrived. For finally Hitler had decided to act and an armoured infantry battalion was on its way from Paulus. According to the radio operator who had received the somewhat garbled message, it was expected to arrive at the bridge by nightfall.

'Let us say at dawn tomorrow, my dear Goldwasser,' he had commented. 'One must always take the statements those field-greys of the Wehrmacht make with a grain of salt!' Goldwasser had seen from the look on the SS officer's face that the thought that they would have to hold out here till the following morning did not worry him particularly.

Now his preparations were complete and his men were enjoying their first hot food for the last twenty-four hours, cooking cans of 'Old Man', the standard meat ration reputedly made of old men, on their entrenching tools held over a petrol-and-earth fire. Harsch and Goldwasser surveyed the big Russian HQ, with the dead lying in confused, frozen heaps in front of it.

'Wonder what's going on over there?' Goldwasser asked thoughtfully, lowering his glasses.

'Yes, me too,' Harsch said. 'They are strangely silent. It's unlike the Popov's. They usually make a great deal of noise before they counter-attack, especially after the political commissars start firing them up and they've swallowed their battle ration of vodka.'

'Perhaps they're not going to attack after all?' Goldwasser suggested.

'It would be a pleasant thought. But what else can they do? Now for them it's either piss or get off the pot. The only alternative they have is surrender — and,' he grinned, 'they'd hardly do that to the armed SS. No, my friend,' he accepted the steaming can of Old Man handed to him by Adolfo gratefully, 'they'll counterattack all right.'

But *Obersturmbannführer* Harsch was wrong. All the fight had gone out of the gulag rats. The beating they had taken at the hands of the Germans had been too much. Now the survivors and wounded lay in the dirty straw, smoking or staring numbly into nothing. All was silence save for the low moaning of the wounded. Even Boldin, the indestructible, slumped in despair, gazing at his blackened hands.

Colonel Katukov frowned. Outside all he could see were shattered bodies, the gory litter of war. All was black, white, blood-red; it was the landscape of absolute despair. He took his gaze off the steppe wolves, knowing that the god of war had finally removed his mask and that the flood gates of ruination had been opened. Yet he still had to act. He couldn't just give up. He must inspire his worn out, savagely beaten scum to one last effort. *He had to*!

He turned slowly and stared around at them lying down on both sides of the room, hardly moving even when the lice started to bite in the heat that came from the green ceiling-high oven. Their bearded faces were hollow-cheeked and had a waiting, wolfish impassivity which came from hardship and want. 'Comrades,' he said simply, using a word that he had never thought fit to apply to the 'scum' from the camps in the long months he had commanded the gulag rats. A couple of heads were raised. The rest remained bent. 'All through history, our land has been defeating invaders,' Katukov continued quietly. 'Our land and our people. Even the Tartars and the Golden Horde couldn't beat us, although it took centuries to break them. But in the end we Russians smashed them all. Livonians, Lithuanians, Poles, the Teutonic Knights, the Swedes, the French. We've always conquered in the end — and we will conquer the Germans, too.'

His words died away hesitantly, but more heads were raised now and Boldin was looking at him curiously, his weary brain trying to understand what was taking place.

'I know you are weary, hurt, desperate even,' Katukov continued, 'but can't you make one last effort? Not for *Stalin*, not for *me*. But for our Russia. For our comrades who are dead out there, who have died all these months since last June for Russia.' Katukov swung his burning gaze around the long room, as if willing them to rise to their feet and obey him. 'Whatever you may have once been, criminals or politicals, you are still Russians. You were conceived in Russian bodies, bred on the fruit of Russian earth, schooled in the Russian tongue.' His voice hardened. 'You have a duty to Russia and to yourselves, to *your* dead, *your* wounded, *your* maimed! You can't overlook that fact, try as you will. And what is that duty, comrades?' He raised his right index finger, his face glowing, his eyes searing their amazed faces. 'I shall tell you. Your sole duty is to carry that bridge. Nothing else. To rise up from the very pit of hell itself. To keep on till death — and beyond death. To take that bridge, rip it from the hands of the obscene fascist beast and give it back to Russia!' He paused, his big chest heaving with the effort of that burning intensity, his eyes noting with a great surge of hope that here and there the weary men were stumbling to their feet and Boldin, their real leader, was fumbling for his equipment. 'It won't be long now, comrades. Then the Red Army will come sweeping down to our aid, a matter of mere hours. But when they come, comrades, we must be waiting for them down at that bridge — even if there is only one of us left — but we must be waiting. *We must!*' He attempted to say more, but the rest of his words were drowned in cheers and suddenly he was in the middle of a mass of men who cried and swore and clapped him on the back, the hated and feared Colonel Katukov. Thus it was that that single dry shot at the bridge was not heard in the wild excitement of the long room.

'*Aee-i-oh*!' Harsch screamed with the absolute agony of it and staggered back against the side of the half-track, broken sword tumbling from his one hand, the fingers pressed up against his shattered right eye suddenly soaked in blood. Before

Goldwasser could reach him, he sat awkwardly on the snow, gasping shallowly with the tremendous pain. High above him, the man from Smersh slung his telescopic rifle and doubled back to the cover of his cave before the German bullets started winging his way. He'd finished the Fritz off for good. He had killed enough men to know the signs of death when he saw them.

Goldwasser tried to prize away the fingers gently, but Harsch held fast as the first terrible wave of pain began to ebb temporarily. 'No good, Goldwasser,' he said weakly. 'This time the Redskin's gonna bite the dust.'

Up at the far end of the bridge his grenadiers started firing wildly in the direction from which the lone shot had come.

'What do you mean?' Goldwasser gasped.

'You ... you're in the SS, Goldwasser, that's what I mean,' Harsch's voice was getting weaker by the instant. 'I hereby pass on the command of the Führer's Fire Brigade to you.' He attempted a smile, but failed lamentably. 'What would Hitler say ... a Jew commanding an SS unit...!' The blood was streaming down between his fingers now and dripping on to his camouflaged blouse.

'But what am I supposed to do?' Goldwasser asked in panic.

'The boys'll see you through... Just hang on, Goldwasser.' Harsch's voice was very weak now. 'Hang on ... till morning... And listen, Goldwasser.' The Italian craned his head forward so that he could hear. 'Once you're safe, take off. Back to Italy... Take a boat from there ... South America ... as far as you can get... Europe's doomed, triple doomed...'

Now the survivors of his elite command were gathered around their dying commander as he lay slumped there in the bloody snow, supported by the little Jew, his chest heaving now in sharp shallow gasps, his good eye almost closed.

'*Mala hora, buena cara*,' the swarthy Adolfo said with pride in this big blonde man whose very language he had hardly understood, but whom he had followed to death. He raised his hand in the Falangist salute.

It acted like a signal.

Frenchman, German, Belgian, Dutchman, Swiss, all of them clicked to attention and their hoarse young voices joined in that fanatical scream to a deity who had long since abandoned them. '*SIEG HEIL ... SIEG HEIL ... SIEG HEIL...*'

On the ground Harsch's head fell to one side, his last words a faint, 'Damned untidy thing to do...'

CHAPTER 6

On the nineteenth of November 1942 at exactly 6.30 a.m. the pre-dawn gloom between the towns of Serafinovich and Kletskaya was transformed suddenly into a brilliant blaze of bright orange and ugly red flame as 3500 Russian cannon of all calibres erupted into violent life. Along the whole winter horizon the brazen lights flickered like angry blast-furnaces and the air was suddenly filled with that obscene, frightening sound of thousands of shells ripping the dawn stillness apart. It was the thunderstroke that opened a major offensive — one that changed the twentieth century. *The march westwards of Soviet Russia had commenced!*

Trapped in their straw-lined trenches and log-roofed dugouts, the fur-hatted Romanians of the Third Army quavered, tight-lipped with fear, as the shells ripped up and down their lines, destroying them metre by metre. The front line, the second line, the reverse line, they all disappeared under the weight of that tremendous bombardment. Bunkers collapsed. Men died fighting the sliding soil. Others went crazy, shouting and singing like village idiots, dancing on their parapets until that whirling, vicious steel maelstrom swept them away. Shell-shocked soldiers screamed soundlessly with terror and buried their ears in their hands; mouths, dripping with crazed saliva, opened purposelessly. Everywhere the telephones whirred as excited, panicked staff officers called for aid. But there was none forthcoming.

One hour later precisely, the tremendous bombardment ceased. There was a loud, echoing silence which died finally in the furthest hills. But not for long. It was soon replaced by the ominous, but certain, rumble of tank tracks. Hundreds of them. Thousands of them. The Russian Fifth and Twenty-first Tank Armies were coming.

'The Ivans are coming ... the Ivans are coming...'

The terrified cry rose everywhere as the first thirty-ton T-34s with the red star on their armoured sides breasted the heights and began churning their way across that lunar landscape, followed by the mass ranks of the Soviet infantry, their brass bands playing military marches, the soldiers linked-armed, goose-stepping towards the Romanian positions in their thousands and hundred thousands, crying *'Urrah Stalino ... Urrah Stalino!'* Drill sergeants dressed their ranks with blows from their swords and the flag-bearers waved that gold and red banner which would bring fear one day to a whole continent as it headed steadily for the English Channel.

The Romanians broke. It was to be expected. As the first T-34s burst out of the fog and snow, they leapt from their shattered trenches and started to run.

On all sides the frightened cry went up. *'Run for it! ... run for it!'*

Priests and cooks, quartermasters and generals packed their trucks and sat in them frantic with fear, praying desperately that their engines would start at last. Then they were off, driving in every direction across that limitless white steppe. Anywhere away from that terrifying Russian steamroller. Corps commanders, soldiers of thirty years' experience, broke down and had to be carried to the waiting staff cars, sobbing like little children. Generals who had often enough in these last terrible years in Russia ordered their men to fight 'to the last soldier and the last cartridge' fled shamefully, leaving their troops to their fate. Others could neither flee nor fight; they were too paralysed by fear. In the end, when the T-34s were already rolling into their headquarters, they put their fancy little pistols into their dry mouths and blew their brains out.

Every man capable of moving was moving now. Even the wounded panicked, crawling across the snow after their comrades, crying piteously, 'Help me, comrade … help me…' No one was listening. But they kept on, the blind using the eyes of the legless, the legless using the legs of the blind.

The Third Romanian Army was broken. Now it was in full retreat, heading for the one bridge across the Don at Kalach.

By midday the Russians are deep into the Romanians' rear.

By the hundred, the T-34s smash in the depots and dumps, their crews looting and drinking as they rolled, leaving blood and crushed bodies and burning, shattered equipment in their wake, their engines going full out, their tracks whining a triumphant song of victory.

A battery of self-propelled guns shell a Romanian cavalry depot and roll through it, plucking at pieces of raw horsemeat and stuffing their mouths full of the bloody flesh so that the grinning gunners with their scarlet, dripping mouths and gleaming white teeth look like cannibals.

A reserve hospital is overrun. For a few moments all goes well, but then the tank infantry find the medical alcohol. Patients are bayoneted on the operating table.

The brown horde sweeps all before it. Here and there a little group of Romanians tries to stop them. To no avail. Red flares hiss into the grey sky everywhere, colouring the snow a blood-red hue. A barrage of unbelievable force sweeps over the heads of the stalled infantry. The mounting thunder of the bombardment flattens the handful of Romanians. In an inferno of flames, flying rubble and earth, and explosions of impossible power, they are ripped apart, clawed from the very ground, whirled upwards to disappear for good in volcanoes of flame.

In the deeper dugouts the Romanians hold out a little longer, but not much. To their front the forest burns as the whirling storm of steel rolls towards them. Men go mad. The dugouts sway to and fro like ships at sea caught in a sudden hurricane. The defenders' eyes are wet with crazed fear. They scream, but no sound comes. And then that terrible maelstrom swamps them too. In its wake, as it passes on, it leaves churned, steaming earth, littered with chunks of human meat.

A Guards' regiment appears out of the snow and mist, legs clad in gleaming jackboots stamping across the snow in perfect step, bayonets gleaming, big bodies proud and packed together, officers with silver sabres across their shoulders, flags flying bravely.

'Fire!' the Romanian colonel cries desperately. His men are all former Iron Guards, the elite of the country. They fire at will.

The Guards are mown down like corn. They come on, automatically closing ranks as they do so, goose-stepping as proudly as ever. The Romanians fire again. Tracer hammers into the Russians. '*Urrah Stalino!*' they cry hoarsely and quicken their pace. A thousand bayonets flash as one. They are going to charge!

The Romanian colonel throws away his pistol. The former Iron Guards break and run. The advance continues.

Between Chir and Kletskaya, General Mihail Lascar surrenders his four divisions, walking through a shattered cavalry unit into captivity.

Hawk-faced General Dumitrescu thinks of shooting himself, but instead the commander of the Third Romanian Army, now a formation in name only, decides he must express his anger to higher headquarters at the way the Germans have let him down. 'Yes, gentlemen,' he cries in feigned rage at his elegant staff. 'The King must hear of this!'

General of the Army Dumitrescu is last seen heading for Bucharest in his gleaming Daimler. The end is not far off now.

It was the mobs of frenzied, unarmed Romanian soldiers who had somehow managed to cross the Don, shellshocked, hysterical, trickling blood from mouth, nose and ears, who first brought the news to the Sixth Army of just how bad the situation was. It travelled speedily through the army right up to Paulus's HQ. Immediately the general's intelligence officers began to work out the details. They were shocking. Of the Third Romanian Army's seven divisions, four had been broken and captured, three had fled. There was nothing now to stop the Red Army sweeping across the Don and cutting off Paulus's left flank. A similar attack on the Romanian Fourth Army to his right would end in the same way. Paulus's Sixth Army ran a serious risk of being cut off to the rear by a great Russian pincer-movement. Now the Russians were turning the German's own blitzkrieg tactics, perfected in France in 1940, against them. An immense debacle of world-shaking importance lay before them if something was not done soon.

General von Paulus woke up at last to his situation. He knew that the Romanians on his left flank were finished and he knew too from Intelligence that along a 200 kilometre front from Beketovka down to the shores of the salt lakes Sarpa, Tzata and Barmantsak that three Soviet armies were massed to attack the vastly overextended Fourth Romanian Army. If he was going to get out, it had to be *now*! The signals requesting an urgent decision flew that morning from Army HQ to Army

Group HQ to that of the Supreme Headquarters until finally they reached Adolf Hitler in the far-off Berghof.

Von Paulus waited and waited. Then finally Hitler's reply was there. He opened it with trembling fingers. If he had known then how much depended upon that signal, his skinny aristocratic body would have trembled, but he didn't.

Speedily his dark eyes ran across the message:

'*Radio message, Number 1352.*
TOP SECRET
Urgent!
To: HQ Sixth Army
Führer Order
Sixth Army will hold positions despite threat of temporary encirclement... Keep railway line open as long as possible. Special orders regarding air supply will follow!'

Wordlessly the tall general passed the message to his chief-of-staff, General Schmidt.

His eyes flew across it. 'But general,' he protested, 'how are they going to supply the army?'

'By air, it appears,' Paulus said looking down at his smaller companion, eyes blank of emotion, though his mind was racing crazily.

'A whole army of a quarter of a million men!' Schmidt exploded. '*Impossible!*'

'It's the Führer's order.'

'I shit on the Führer!' Schmidt burst out, exasperated beyond measure, his gross face flushed with rage. 'In the filthy weather we have here there isn't a hope in hell of supplying us by air. Look, it's snowing again. *By air!* general, *it's stark, staring madness!*'

'It's the Führer's order,' von Paulus repeated as if the words were part of some ancient liturgy.

The Sixth Army was doomed. As Churchill was to say, 'The hinge of fate had turned.'

CHAPTER 7

The massed fire of the two half-tracks stopped the gulag rats dead. The first line was simply wiped off the face of the earth, disappearing into the smoke of the chattering 20mm cannon and hissing, massed machine-guns. The second line flung themselves to the body-littered ground, clawing at the snow with their hands, frantically trying to bury themselves, get away from that terrible merciless fire.

Katukov, his chest heaving wildly, blood pouring from a deep gash at his temple, dropped into a steaming hole next to Boldin, and gasped, 'We didn't pull it off ... we didn't pull it off!' His head bent, that once proud man, as broken now as the scum who had followed him so bravely a few minutes before, sobbed as if his heart were broken.

Gravely Boldin patted his heaving shoulder. 'You tried, comrade, you tried,' he whispered, trying at the same time to place the strange rumble that was beginning to come from their rear. 'What can mere men do against armoured positions like that?'

Katukov continued to sob. He was a broken man.

Boldin bit his bottom lip. He had seen it before. Katukov's nerve had gone. He would never be any good any more. His days as a soldier were over. Colonel Katukov would never again command a combat formation.

Boldin flashed a look around the survivors of the second wave. They were absolutely beaten. Around their cracked lips, the flesh quivered and their eyes were glazed with an unnatural sheen. They would not attack again this day. The gulag rats were a spent force.

The strange rumble was getting louder, but Major Boldin was only just aware of it. Suddenly he was overcome by an unreasoning rage at the sobbing Katukov and the worn, exhausted men lying and crouching in the snow all around him. He forced himself to his feet, ignoring the first slugs that came howling his way from the German positions. 'On your idle feet, you shit-shovelling scum!' he roared.

No one moved. 'Comrade major,' someone protested.

'Couldn't get up a whore's drawers, even if she was lying on her back with her legs spread in the air,' someone else said wearily, voice full of bitter humour.

'You dogs!' Major Boldin cried, sobbing with rage, the slugs cutting the air around him, '*You rats of the gulag, do you want to live for ev —*'

Boldin stopped short.

Over the heights to their rear, there were running men in fur hats, locked together with trucks and horse-drawn carts — hundreds of them, thousands of them. Men flogging ponies furiously. Others grabbing for the running boards of the trucks. All shouting.

Sweating, swearing, screaming, the first of the drivers came closer, lashing their snow-caked ponies, already frothing at the mouth, the carts disgorging their contents as other soldiers threw overboard the loot of a year in Russia, leaving a trail of litter behind them over which the men on foot fell.

'Romanians — *counter-attack!*' someone screamed.

Wearily the gulag rats grabbed for their weapons, knowing now that nothing could save them. There were thousands of the enemy out there. They would be swamped.

But they were not witnessing an attack, but a stampede as the Romanians streamed by the open-mouthed gulag rats, shouldering them, pushing them out of the way, hardly aware they were there at all in their haste to get across the bridge, running for their lives, passing over debris, dreams and dead, over the tears of those who had suffered and died for this bit of Russian earth, with history following in their wake. For behind them roared the steel might of the Red Army, the armoured mass of the T-34s. The gulag rats would need to attack the bridge at Kalach no more.

Half an hour later it was all over.

Against the side of the bridge they were shooting the SS; they always did. Their last cries rang out in the language of all of Western Europe, as if the old continent was saying its good-bye. They were brave, banal and bawdy. '*Maricons... Es lebe Deutschland... De koffie ist klaar ... figlio di puttana... Arschloch ... merde...*' Western Europe died on that bridge that November day.

Not that the gulag rats cared or even listened. They celebrated. There was an accordion and vodka. They played the music and the Rats and the men of the Red Army danced together. Bags filled with delicacies were handed out to them, cakes smeared with chocolate frosting, chocolate bars, biscuits, tins of pork. Every new tank ploughing its way through the piles of Romanian dead which lined both sides of the traffic-choked road, had packets of cigarettes for them and bottles of looted Romanian red wine. It was a feast the likes of which the bearded, exhausted veterans had not seen these many years. But like all feasts it had to end.

And it ended with a shock.

The civilian with the straight, lustreless hair and the frightening, hanging hands covered with thick black hairs, wasted no time. 'Colonel Katukov?' he rapped.

Katukov looked up, his face still blank and wet with tears, he stared unseeingly at the civilian, backed up by the platoon of Greenhats armed with tommy guns. He said nothing.

'Who are you? What do you want?' Boldin spoke for him.

The civilian did not take his flat, impenetrable eyes off Katukov.

'Is this him?' he asked.

'Katukov? ... yes.'

The man from Smersh held up his ID card with that dreaded name printed underneath it for all to see, 'S-M-E-R-S-H' as if that were explanation enough. 'Take him away...' he commanded.

ENVOI: *THE DESTRUCTION OF COLONEL KATUKOV*

'The celebrated tale of the man who gave the powder to the bear. He mixed the powder with the greatest care, making sure that not only the ingredients but the proportions were absolutely correct. He rolled it up in a large paper spill and was about to blow it down the bear's throat. *But the bear blew first.'*
Winston Churchill — *The Second World War*

Katukov squatted in the corner of the big cell, watching one of the prisoners whittle the frozen black bread into equal portions. He was no longer hungry, but the others, a mixed bunch of deserters, cowards who had refused to attack, officers relieved of their commands because of incompetency, were desperate for food. They never took their eyes off the man carving and stabbing at the precious bread. As if it were very important to stay alive, Katukov told himself wearily. They would all hang or be shot by the NKVD before the week was out.

Katukov turned his gaze to the cone-shaped mound of excrement in the corner. It had risen slowly, recording the length of the condemned men's stay in the cell, and it was always black, the colour of the frozen bread, their only food.

Outside, the thunder of the guns had diminished and Katukov could hear the NKVD guards opening the doors of the cells further down the long corridor and crying, '*Skolko kaput?'*

'How many dead?' Katukov mused. They had three propped up in the shadows of the corner of their cell. At first some of his fellow prisoners had been for throwing them out, but Petrov, the general who had abandoned his division when it had been ordered across the Volga into the hell of Stalingrad, had pointed out that frigid temperatures within the cell would keep the bodies from decomposing for weeks and thus they would be able to get extra rations of bread. Katukov had sniffed, 'For weeks!' but the others hadn't listened. They had been too hungry.

So now he sat among the starving, the shit, and the dead, and mused on his fate.

There had not even been a court-martial. The man from Smersh had had him led into Chuikov's office and declared simply, 'Katukov, the man from Kalach.'

Helplessly, he had stared at Chuikov's seamed, tough face, but the commanding general had avoided his gaze. Instead he had asked of the man from Smersh, 'What is your decision?'

'Comrade Beria had ordered —' the man from Smersh did not finish his sentence. Instead he turned his thumb down in the classical symbol. Chuikov had nodded. 'So be it.'

'But,' Katukov had begun and then he had closed his mouth and, head hanging miserably, had allowed himself to be led away. That had been the extent of his 'trial'.

Now he had been in the cell with these contemptuous creatures for five days. It couldn't be much longer before they came for him with that '*Davoi* bistre' which meant the end.

The man handed him his iron-hard piece of bread, holding his free hand underneath the sliver carefully, ensuring that any crumb that might fall off would not be wasted. Katukov thanked him gravely; he wanted nothing to do with these wretches. Hardly aware that he was doing so, he started to chew on the bread, his mind blank of all thought save for that one overwhelming question: *when?*

It was the same question that Boldin and Vulf were asking themselves, as they watched the hangman, 'The Tuliak' (he came from Tula) supervise the erection of the gallows half a kilometre from the cell where their former commander lay.

Behind them the din was tremendous as the bulldozers from America rattled back and forth, their cruel scoops biting into the piles of dead, German and Russian, raising them high into the air for a moment before depositing them in the great open graves like heaps of logs, whereupon emaciated German POWs with handkerchiefs tied across their mouths started to sprinkle the bodies with quicklime.

Tuliak was not a small man. Indeed he stood just short of one metre ninety, with a chest like that of a carthorse. He was completely bald with a pair of unbelievably wicked eyes, blazing like searchlights above his vodka-thickened nose. Now he swaggered back and forth, chewing on a piece of dried meat, shouting his orders at the soldier carpenters, a small piece of rope between his reddened hams, playing with it all the time like a Muslim with his 'prayer beads', as if it gave him a feeling of security, satisfaction, to have the tool of his trade always with him.

'A pig,' Vulf commented, 'a real pig.'

Boldin nodded, sizing up the hangman, wondering how they could get to him. Katukov had been vain, ambitious, and often harsh and cruel to that scum which he detested, the gulag rats. Still, he did not deserve to die in this ignoble manner — at the end of Tuliak's hempen rope. 'What did you hear of him?' he asked finally, raising his voice as a fresh battery opened up across the Don at the Germans now trapped in a dying Stalingrad.

Vulf shrugged. 'I don't know why you bother. But I will tell you all the same. Professional killer. Back in the bad times in the late twenties. Mostly women. Throttled them for food.'

Boldin looked at the hangman with his brutally muscled shoulders which rippled even through the thick, wadded civilian jacket. 'Pleasant sort of a fellow, eh, Vulf?'

Vulf nodded and shuddered as those red hams unconsciously twisted the rope once more, feeling for the knot which would be placed just beneath the victim's Adam's apple.

'How did the NKVD find him?'

'He got caught and was sent to the gulag. As you know, Boldin, the so-liberal Soviet State got rid of the death penalty for murder back in those days.' He sneered. They only shot you for saying the sun didn't shine out of Stalin's arse or something as heinous as that. After a while Beria heard of his — er — talents, and selected him as the NKVD's chief hangman to be used when it was necessary to make a public example of some traitor or the like. Just as our former commander is going to be made one *pour encourager les autres*, as the frogs say.' He spat into the dirty snow. 'The pigs!'

'Yes,' Boldin said slowly, pondering Vulf's contemptuous words. 'So friend Tuliak was once in the gulag... He knows the rules... Hmm.' He took Vulf by the arm and led him away through the masses of fresh infantry laden like pack mules who were preparing to cross the Volga for the final battle with von Paulus's trapped Germans, now all but gone to ground in the smoking rubble that had once been Stalin's own city.

'What are you thinking, Boldin?' Vulf asked as they walked slowly towards the gulag rats' lines, guarded as always when they were out of action by surly NKVD men, armed with Maxim machine-guns.

Boldin did not answer his question directly. Instead he said, 'I know you don't like Katukov.'

'To be frank, I've *hated* the bastard with a passion at times,' Vulf broke in.

Boldin didn't seem to hear. 'But whatever his faults, Katukov is a brave man who has fought all his life for Russia, however misguided his other motives might have been.'

Vulf halted and looked directly at Boldin. 'Listen, have you had your hundred? How can we get Katukov out of a NKVD jail in the middle of this armed camp?'

'Even if you could convince the rest of the gulag rats to follow you in the attempt, which I doubt, what good would those couple of hundred exhausted men be against the thousands of troops here? There must be at least two regiments of NKVD alone. Now tell me that, Boldin!'

The big ex-marshal grinned down at the little man, the thin rays of the winter sun sparkling on Boldin's stainless steel teeth, obviously amused at his companion's genuine anger. 'Who said anything about getting Katukov out of jail?' he said mysteriously. 'What do we need to do that for when we've got the Tuliak...'

The Tuliak lay on a hard wooden bed next to the roaring tiled oven, his ugly face red with the tremendous heat. He prised a piece of meat from between his teeth with a bayonet. He was alone in the dugout although even general officers had to double up in the crowded rear echelon lines; but then he was the Tuliak of the NKVD. Ten minutes went by before he condescended to notice the two grubby private soldiers, devoid of any badges of rank or unit identification, standing just inside the blanket-covered doorway to the underground dugout. 'Well, what do you two evil maggots want?' he asked at last, swinging himself up from his bed and dropping his bayonet, instinctively reaching for that short length of rope.

'Not much, just a few words with you, Tuliak,' the bigger of the two soldiers answered. Calmly he walked across the room and, picking up the rest of the meat lying on the greasy plate, stuffed it in his own mouth, while his companion, holding some sort of bundle in his hand, grinned maliciously through his thick, horn-rimmed spectacles.

The hangman's mouth flopped open stupidly. He gasped hard, as if someone had just punched him in his fat overhanging gut. 'What ... what do you think you're up to?' he roared in a vodka-tinged bass, his wicked, coal-black eyes blazing. 'Don't you red-arsed monkeys know who I am!... I'm not just anybody.' He stood up, towering even above the big private soldier and jerked a thumb at his massive chest, '*I'm the devil himself*.'

The man who had stolen Tuliak's supper was unimpressed. He swallowed the rest of the meat and said quite calmly, 'I'll show you something ... devil.' He reached in the pocket of his earth-coloured soldier's blouse and brought out an object which glittered a bright silver in the wavering light of the candles that illuminated the dugout. 'Razor-blade,' he said and placed the thing in his mouth. He crunched hard and began chewing, almost as if he enjoyed it, while Tuliak stared at him, his brutish face a mixture of wonder and disbelief.

There was a trick of doing it without any harm but Tuliak did not know that. He was obviously impressed as the big soldier carefully spat out sliver after sliver of chewed steel, thrusting out his tongue at intervals to reveal it was whole, before finally reaching over and taking a swig out of the hangman's own bottle of vodka.

'What ... what do you want from me?' he said, not as confident as he had been a few moments before.

'I have been told you are a good sort of fellow and like to help people,' the soldier who had chewed the razor-blade said.

'What?'

'You heard.'

'You cheeky arse with ears!' Tuliak thundered. 'Don't you know that even the felt-lice don't even dare move in the Tuliak's shitty drawers during the great man's rest hours and you barn-shitters dare come in...' His words drained away as he saw the object which the one with glasses was displaying inside the handkerchief that he had just unfolded. '*Boshe moi*!...' he croaked, 'is ... is that...?'

'It is,' the little man said calmly. He walked across the dugout and deposited it on the packing-case which served as a table.

'That ... *that's a sawn-off cock*!' he stuttered stupidly. 'A human cock...' He swallowed hard and stared down at the bloody piece of flesh which lay in the cloth.

The little man nodded. 'Yes ... it could be yours.'

The Tuliak started back. '*Mine?*' he quavered.

'Yes, if you don't prove just how good you really are,' the big man said, making a cutting gesture.

The Tuliak shuddered. 'But who are you?... What do you want from me?'

'Sit down,' the big one said and he pressed the Tuliak back on to his wooden bench. 'I've got something to explain to you, little brother, something very important. If you wish to keep your salami, unlike the poor fool to whom that one belonged, you'd better listen and listen carefully.'

The Tuliak listened.

The man from Smersh was pleased with himself. Beria had signalled his congratulations. Perhaps there might be some of those first-class trips abroad for him again after all. Now he waited for the night train which would take him away from Stalingrad back to the comparative safety of Moscow. He no longer had any interest in Katukov. Chuikov would take care of him; he wouldn't dare fail.

Impatiently, he stamped his feet on the cold concrete and wished the goods train would make its appearance. Chuikov had reserved a whole carriage for him just behind the engine. There would be steam-heating and, knowing just how much the military brass feared Smersh, probably a hamper of food, vodka and wine as well. He eyed the common soldiers, most of them lightly wounded, who thronged everywhere, waiting for the train. What a miserable existence they led, he told himself and thanked a god he didn't believe in once again, that the Soviet system had given him the opportunity it had.

'Comrade!'

The man from Smersh spun round.

A common soldier was standing there under the faint blue light of the blacked-out platform lantern, grinning at him with a mouthful of stainless steel teeth, his right arm in a dirty, blood-stained sling. 'What do you want?' he asked coldly, disliking being called 'comrade' by this dirty foot-slogger.

The soldier indicated the unlit cigarette, a roughly made compound of black tobacco and newspaper. 'A light, comrade.'

'A light ... oh, yes.' He had been about to refuse, but now the goods train was beginning to steam slowly into the station, its floodlight illuminating the snow-bound track, and he didn't want to be detained by the soldier's whining importunings if he refused. 'Here,' he fumbled inside his thick fur jacket and brought out a box of matches.

'Could you light it for me, comrade,' the soldier had the cheek to ask. 'Bit difficult with my one flipper, you see.'

'Damn… All right, come closer!'

'Many thanks, comrade.' Obediently the soldier moved closer and, striking the match, the man from Smersh reached up to light the cigarette for the soldier.

It was then that he saw clearly the soldier's face, those bold eyes and broad cheeks. 'Hey aren't you —'

His scream of agony was drowned by the clatter of the goods train's locked wheels, as the razor-sharp dagger that Boldin had carried in the sling in the fashion of the gulag killer slid deep into his stomach. Then he was falling, falling, falling, his skin seared by the heat of the red-hot boiler before the great, gleaming, cruel steel wheel ran right over him.

A moment later Boldin had gone, slipping through the excited, curious, unfeeling mob of soldiers, disappearing into the night to where Vulf had the horse waiting for him.

The man from Smersh had committed his last murder…

The battalions, to which the criminals who were now going to be publicly hanged had once belonged, were lined up around the gallows. They were formed in a hollow square, sunk in a hushed, dawn silence, the new snow falling softly on their bent, great-coated shoulders.

On the raised platform with its twelve nooses, the Tuliak, arms crossed across his massive chest, waited impassively, head framed by one evil circle of hemp. The kettledrums rolled softly. The hangings could commence.

The senior NKVD officer in his green-cross cap, now powdered with snow, raised the charge sheet, his other hand grasping his sabre. 'Former General of the Infantry Petrov.

Accused of cowardice in the field. Sentence — death by hanging!'

The kettledrums started to beat quicker.

'Division Petrov — *eyes left!*' the NKVD officer rapped.

The two hundred or so men representing the division which the general had deserted snapped their heads to the left. Petrov, his head uncovered, chin thrown out proudly, hands tied behind his back, came stalking out into the cobbled courtyard, guarded by riflemen of his own division, his last escort. He was shivering, whether from fear or cold, no one would ever know. Guided by his former soldiers, he mounted the steps to where the Tuliak was waiting for him.

As the drum beat increased, the hangman untied his bonds and swiftly threw the noose over the general's head, adjusting the big knot so that it lay to the left of the victim's Adam's apple. The general waited impassively. The wind strengthened. More and more snow started to fall on his erect shoulders. The NKVD officer nodded to the Tuliak. He pulled the lever.

Snap! There was a startled gasp from the soldiers. Suddenly the general was dangling there, the rope twisting under the impact, his head bent grotesquely, his tongue hanging out of the side of his mouth like a piece of wet leather, his trousers at the front black with urine. General of the Infantry Petrov was dead!

Immediately the NKVD photographers rushed forward. Their flashes cut the gloom as they recorded the event for the Red Army's official newspapers. Even in this month of victory, those who wavered had been shown the dread results of such hesitation.

'Former Captain of the Guards Manitskov. Accused of military failure in the field. Sentence — death by hanging!' the

NKVD officer read out, the snowflakes shrouding his shoulders now.

'No, no' the tall captain cried, 'I don't want to die... *No, please don't*'

The two guardsmen grabbed their ex-commander more firmly and half-pushed, half-dragged him to where the Tuliak stood waiting for him at the second gallows, arms crossed as before. The drum beat increased. Everywhere the soldiers dropped their eyes save in the Guards Regiment where again the soldiers clicked their heads woodenly to the left to observe the last march of ex-Captain Manitskov. The snow pelted down.

Thus the gruesome public hanging continued with wretch after wretch being dragged through the snow by former subordinates or comrades to finish dangling and swaying at the end of one of Tuliak's hemp ropes.

Now there were eleven of them swaying there, almost obscured by the flying snow which was coming down as if it would never stop again, as if God himself wanted to blot out that cruel misery below.

'Ex-Colonel Katukov of the 333rd Punishment Battalion!' the NKVD officer bellowed, the wind snatching at his words. 'Accused of grave disobedience in the field. Sentence — death by hanging!'

The drums rolled as two gulag rats, one tall and burly, the other skinny and undersized, dragged out the Tuliak's last victim, the big form somehow shrunken, his head lolling, as if he were already unconscious. Indeed a third gulag rat, a big fellow, whose features were obscured by the flying snow, hurried into the courtyard to aid the other two as they virtually carried their victim to the gallows.

'Punishment Battalion — *eyes left!*' the NKVD officer rapped and there was no mistaking the contempt in his voice at the craven manner in which Katukov, a former NKVD officer himself, was going to meet his death. A Greenhat was supposed to be above fear, at least in public. His contempt was reflected in the faces of some of the gulag rats as they watched their commander being led to his death.

Then finally the three gulag rats got him on to the gallows where they were forced to support him until the Tuliak had his rope around Katukov's bent neck. He rapped, 'Stand back there,' and pulled the trap hastily.

The dead man dropped like a sack of cement.

The hangings were over. The drums beat. The lone bugle sounded. Sabres flashed. Officers bellowed orders and the regiments marched off, their boots muffled by the snow, leaving the dead to hang there in the streaming white, a grim warning to all who might pass this way to the battle on the other side of the Don. Stalin's revenge was terrible…

'Cheer up, colonel,' Vulf said, as the three of them squatted in the cover of a wrecked T-34, waiting for the goods train to come along the single line below, already blocked by the trees they had placed across it. 'It all worked out well.'

'I am no longer a colonel,' the man in the long civilian overcoat, complete with cloth cap, said sadly. 'I am nobody. A faceless one.'

Boldin did not take his eyes off the railway line, save occasionally to flash a glance at the green-glowing dial of his wristwatch. The train heading out of Stalingrad with its freight of damaged weapons being carried to the repair workshops to the rear of Stalingrad was due any minute now. During the daylight hours the line was dead on account of the Fritz dive-bombers; the driver would want to get clear of the embattled city before it was too light.

The escape had worked out well. The Tuliak had been convinced easily enough — after he had seen that sawn-off penis — that he was dealing with two killers who would take their revenge even if it meant their own death to do so; he had been in the gulag long enough to know the type. Thereafter it had been simply a matter of ensuring that Katukov would be the last one to be hanged. The Tuliak, scared out of his skin, had gone along with everything so that it had not been difficult for Vulf and himself to slip Katukov, the last man in the cell, a common soldier's cap, while they grabbed one of the three corpses there to take his place. The only hitch had been Katukov's weak protest, 'But I want to die ... I deserve to die ... I disobeyed orders.'

Boldin's quick, angry, 'We're risking our lives to get you out of this hell-hole, Katukov, so don't play the fool!' had swiftly brought him to his senses. He had hurried after them as they had dragged 'Colonel Katukov' to his death.

Now they were carrying out the last stage of the escape. In a matter of minutes while the train crew cleared away the 'fall', they would slip Katukov on the train heading eastwards. He had a civilian pass they had taken from one of the dead and sufficient money to give him a start. Yet Boldin could see from Katukov's face that he wasn't happy.

'What will I do?' Katukov asked miserably. 'I know only the trade of soldiers. The army has been my life... What will I do? The square, the discipline, the orders, the tramp of marching feet, the smell of polished leather and gleaming steel,' he rambled on numbly, 'it's been my ... whole life. I know no other. *The flag...*' He broke off abruptly.

Listening to the big, broken man, Boldin felt a sudden icy cold, the awful loneliness, the silence, the desolation of this winter world in which they all lived and it made him angry to feel thus. 'Dammit, Katukov,' he blurted out, 'that's all over, don't you realize? You're an outcast like we are outcasts. The system has condemned us! We have no home, no family, no fatherland anymore! *No flag!*' He flashed Katukov a bitter look, his eyes blazing angrily. 'Katukov, you have become that which you have always despised and hated — now *you* are a gulag rat, every man's hand against you, condemned to wander across the face of a fatherland that does not want you until death finally and mercifully releases you from this living hell!'

'Me ... *a gulag rat*.' Katukov quavered and somehow, though it might have been a trick of the grey pre-dawn light, his once proud face seemed to shrink, become hollow-cheeked, with the eyes suddenly cunning, almost shifty, yet bold and knowing like those wolfish prison faces to be found everywhere in the 333rd Punishment Battalion.

Five minutes later when the train squealed rustily to a halt down below, and the driver and his mate, used to this sort of thing, but angry at the extra work all the same, set about clearing away the logs, cursing at each other as they did so, Katukov stole into the rear wagon noiselessly and concealed himself expertly beneath the tarpaulin over a wrecked howitzer, as if he had been doing this sort of thing all his life. He had indeed become a gulag rat...

A thousand and a half kilometres away, *Reichsmarschall* Hermann Göring thundered in his bombastic style over the airways, spitting out the words which no one in Stalingrad listened to anymore; for now the thousands of hungry, weary, ragged Germans who were struggling out of their cellars and throwing away their weapons were prisoners. Stalingrad had just surrendered, making those pompous phrases that crackled over the loudspeakers, hung everywhere in the ruins, sound ironic, absurd, mocking.

'Rising above all these gigantic battles like a mighty monument is Stalingrad... One day this will be recognized as the greatest battle in our history ... a battle of heroes ... We have a mighty epic ... the struggle of the Nibelungs... My soldiers, thousands of years have passed and thousands of years ago in a tiny pass in Greece stood a brave and bold man with three hundred soldiers, Leonidas with his three hundred Spartans... Then the last man fell and now only the inscription stands... "Wanderer, if you should come to Sparta, go tell the Spartans you found us lying here as the law bade us"... Someday men will read, "If you come to Germany, go tell the Germans you saw us lying in Stalingrad, as the law bade us"...'

But there would be few of those who surrendered this January day who would return to tell Germany what had happened. At the Univermag Building, 3000 moaning, cursing German wounded lay in a merciless wind that whipped through the shattered walls, with the helpless doctors placing the most seriously ill at the edge of the packed crowd so that they would die first from the cold.

Ringing the huge brick building on four sides was a stack of frozen corpses two metres high, past which the mournful, groaning lines of German prisoners in their thousands shuffled without a single glance. Lowing like cattle, dilapidated earmuffs over their ears, their heads wrapped in blankets, their faces blackened by beards and frost, they were urged eastwards by the little Siberians on their ponies who cracked their cruel, leaded whips whenever the long column appeared to be stopping, marching to their deaths.

Then the air was filled with another sound — the stamp of well-trained infantry going the other way. Hastily, the Siberians cracked their whips and herded their prisoners to one side. A new battalion with a difference. Next to Colonel Boldin, there fluttered the black skull and-crossbones of the 333rd Punishment Battalion, reinforced and back to its old strength: 800 men from the camps, saints and sinners, faces set as they marched westwards to fight and die for the Kremlin tyrant who aimed to conquer the world.

Here and there some of the soldiers watched those dense ranks, following the big colonel astride his grey mare next to that sinister flag. Some of the watchers crossed themselves in awe; others spat and looked away as if they could not bear to see the scum of the camps; a few whispered in subdued tones, 'It's the rats, the gulag rats!'

But it was one of the Siberians, who gave them the name by which they would be remembered in Stalingrad long after the last one of them was dead. 'Not gulag rat,' he said in his strange Siberian sing-song. 'No, they ... steppe wolves ... understand.' He pointed a skinny finger at the soldiers disappearing up the street into the softly falling snow, *wolves of the steppe...*'

A NOTE TO THE READER

Dear Reader,

If you have enjoyed this novel enough to leave a review on **Amazon** and **Goodreads**, then we would be truly grateful.

Sapere Books

Sapere Books is an exciting new publisher of brilliant fiction and popular history.

To find out more about our latest releases and our monthly bargain books visit our website:
saperebooks.com